This story is a work of fiction. Name
incidents are fictitious and any simil
locations, or events is coincidental.

ISBN: 978-1-998763-34-4

HATEFUL PITCHES

LEO X. ROBERTSON

THE MOTH & FLAME

As Oliver Baring emerged from the darkness, in all his infamy, Ben dropped the waiter's hand.

Dad steepled his fingers. "Happy Birthday!"

His rasping voice implied "London Dad", Ben's moniker for the slimy character that possessed his father. You heard it in the tone of his voice, saw it in the slick of his hair, the snarl of his teeth. London Dad took over every business trip when the landing gear hit Heathrow's tarmac.

"Thanks Dad." Ben held out a hand, not sure if it was a handshake or hug. Dad just looked at him, no sign of standing up. Ben patted his shoulder twice, eliciting a grin.

Dad shimmered, his hair slicked back, sharp profile of his face lined with light from candles on the table. The appearance of health, to Oliver Baring, meant looking like every free surface of him was thinly coated in oil.

He raised a flute of champagne. There was a bottle of it on the table. Empty cocktail glasses, too. Dad had started before Ben's arrival.

Way before.

The waiter, who had introduced himself as Luis, pulled out a chair. As Ben took a seat—thick leather, perfect firmness—he drank in his surroundings. Once a bank in the eighteenth century, they'd kept the marble columns, domed ceiling and original fireplaces. Not that you could see much of anything. Lit only by candles, there was a dream-like smoky haze in the air. Windows on the building front flooded the place with light during the day. Nothing but Hyde Park before them.

Worth outing myself as Oliver Baring's son?

Well, their fellow Moth & Flame clientele—all in tuxes and elegant evening dresses, turning their heads towards Oliver Baring when possible—they were media cunts too, weren't they? They'd known what Dad was up to. They just couldn't 'open secret' it now that so many victims had come forward.

Speaking of which, even Ben could recognize Jasmine Blackwood at a table up the back. Dark skin, long black hair in a high ponytail, dress of silver paillettes.

As Ben met her eyes, she looked hurriedly back to her dining companions.

Ben took the champagne bottle, pouring himself a glass.

Dad swallowed loudly. "Isabella sends her regards."

Dad had introduced her as his secretary. She was obviously more than that. Or less, even. The rail-thin model, forty years Dad's junior, was constantly inebriated—and too in the throes of some horrible eating disorder—to function well enough for any job. "Don't you think," she'd slurred at Ben last he'd met her, "Heaven is an endless line of cocaine?"

"Pass on my thanks when you next see her," Ben replied, quaffing his champagne.

Dad, so comfortable in his Isabella implications, must have left Ben's mum.

So he guessed. Dad wouldn't say more and Mum never asked questions. About Isabella, the rumors—nothing. The Baring family were, despite being Scottish, quite British—a different thing entirely—in their inability to discuss anything of substance.

To keep himself quiet, and soak up some of the already excessive alcohol—champagne straight to his head, Ben studying so hard, drinking so little—he reached for the bread basket. The bread glistened with freshness. He dipped a piece in a plate of olive oil, dotted with black blots of vinegar, and stuffed it in his mouth.

The student in him wanted to fill up his stomach—and perhaps pockets—so he didn't spend too much. But when it came to Dad's company, excess was perhaps the *only* point.

Luis returned with wine bottles and glasses on a polished metal tray.

Dewy olive skin. Top knot of thick black hair. Cool ornate tattoos that dipped into his shirt.

Ben had dreaded dinner with Dad, but Luis had made

a great first impression. Surely why he'd been hired. Rich older men must have gone nuts for this strapping twenty-something and his deep brown eyes.

Since the lack of light had disoriented Ben at first, Luis had held his hand out for Ben to take as he led him through the restaurant to his dad.

Who does that? He likes me!

Ben smiled up at Luis, who winked back at him.

Ben assumed his dad was too busy thinking about himself to be actively prejudiced against anyone, but he didn't want to push it by flirting with the waiter. Only Dad, with respect to the female service staff, had that privilege.

Luis placed the tray down at the table's edge and took out a golden comb and matching business card-sized plate. He brushed bread debris off the cream tablecloth.

How sexy, this pretentious ritual! Ben pictured Luis cleaning the toilet of his pokey student flat with his toothbrush. Luis polishing Ben's 'interview brogues' with his tongue. Luis—*sucking the poison from my battle wounds? What the fuck is wrong with me?*

Luis showed a wine bottle label to Ben's dad, "For Sir, we have a 2018 Malbec from the *Adrianna* Vineyard," his accent inflected with Spanish towards the end.

Dad, as standard, resented the interruption. He glanced at the label as Luis poured a little for him to swish around.

"Comes to you," Luis continued, "all the way from the Gualtallary region of Mendoza in Argentina. As do I!" He smiled, cringily awaiting interest from Oliver in this personal tidbit.

It never came. Oliver eyed him with practiced disdain, like he was a scarecrow that had just learned how to talk.

"Oh!" Ben exclaimed in s weak attempt to put Luis at ease. He hoped Dad's attitude towards servers wasn't enough to turn Luis off *him* too.

Luis winked at Ben *again*.

Are Argentinians just matey like that? More hands-on than most? And I'm just misreading everything?

Nevertheless, Ben planned to write—not his phone number, but the more innocuous-seeming social media handles, on the bill when it eventually arrived. Here in London, in this day and age, he wouldn't even be the only guy making an attempt on Luis this evening.

Dad tasted the wine and nodded.

Luis poured him a large glass. "A full-bodied wine. Notes of dark fruit and spices. It'll go great with your steak." He picked up a second bottle, white this time. "For Sir Number Two, a German Riesling with a unique sweetness that'll pair expertly with the swordfish."

"But we haven't ordered yet." Ben scanned through the menu—thick, hardbound, curly font printed on rough cream paper. No prices in sight, just endless French.

Dad's face fell. "You used to love fish and chips as a boy."

Ben should have learned by now that, like everything, Dad would take this personally.

Luis interjected. "I can go check with—"

"Stay where you are!" Dad barked.

Ben downed his sip of wine without tasting it and nodded to get a full glass. Anything to ensure Luis' quick departure.

As Luis walked away, he fired one last wink at Ben. Ben absorbed this before turning to Dad, whose face had gone grim. Ben must have had, in his expression, the delight of flirtation. If Dad disapproved of queerness—he was silent on the topic, not promising in itself—he might've picked a restaurant that didn't face one of the biggest gay cruising hotbeds in the city.

Dad snapped back into charm mode. "To my son on his twenty-fourth year!" He raised his glass. "To success in his upcoming exams in…?"

"Machine learning."

Ben was in London for uni, Dad for business. The exams were over, just the thesis left, but Ben wasn't about to correct Oliver Baring. He didn't even feel comfortable taking an evening off his studies, far behind as he constantly felt.

"Too clever for me, all that!" Dad said. "Just happy

to fund it."

Even happier to bring it up!

Could be the only good thing the guy *had* done. Yet how many problems in life avoided, how many opportunities afforded through the magic of throwing money at them?

The main course's arrival provided a welcome intermission from their cringeworthy repartee. Here was Luis with Dad's ribeye steak, roast potatoes and truffle butter. He delivered the plate with a flourish and a final twist to make sure the restaurant's logo faced Dad properly.

And here came Ben's swordfish with the same panache. It arrived in two big steaks, with shimmering silvery skin, coated in black crosshatches from the grill.

Ben drank his Riesling, suppressing his sour reaction, replacing it with a fake smile. "So, Dad. Read any good scripts lately?"

These words, from his own lips! Who would have thought it?

How many desperate, shaky, nervy, nerdy young white men he'd witnessed—the kids of famous directors they'd attached to their crap, the nephews of some star who'd agreed to an appearance—clutching sweat-warped papers filled with sad little quips and tedious turning points, pawing at Oliver Baring for approval!

"God," Dad said, sipping champagne, "there's this

one floating around that everyone's going wild about. God knows why! It'll never make money. It's tragic, vile and just plain weird."

Ben drummed his fingers on the table. "Sounds like I'd love it!"

"Forgot you were part of that A24 generation." Dad waved his hands in the air mockingly. "The weirder, the better!"

Ben pinched at the septum of his nose, a nervous habit he had when he needed a small jolt of pain to focus himself. "Maybe you'd like to tell me what it's about."

"I wouldn't like to dwell on such sordid material," he said. "But sure, I can summarise. *Confidentially*, of course."

ADIEU, TRISTESSE

Thomas' students poured into the annex to celebrate him getting his shit together.

Low ceiling, fluorescent strip lights. A punch bowl of diluting juice watered to flavourless yellow nothing. Sandwiches of stale white bread coated in Nutella. No specific party supplies, just leftover materials from the after-school club, for kids of parents who couldn't pick them up straight away.

Rohit, Siddharth and Avi, the Indian boys, were first to arrive as usual.

Andrius and Emilija, the Lithuanians, came in holding hands! Thomas had assumed they were dating already, because they were the only Lithuanians. Turned out they'd met through his club! Had he accidentally set them up? Would he one day be responsible for little Baltic babies?

No sign of Zahra, his favourite. He knew why, but it was still sad.

"We're carrying on the club by the way," Andrius told him, unable to stop smiling for once. One of those manly men, well-built, constantly dressed in hiking gear, even if just going to school.

"Still meet every Wednesday," Emilija added. "Even

though you're leaving us!" She too, perhaps in homage of her new boyfriend, looked ready to scale a mountain.

Since it was Thomas' last day, he dressed as he had done at the weekends. Cloth harem pants, tight t-shirt. Long hair loose, straggly beard unkempt. He'd donned his favourite leather jewellery, the bits with the pewter shapes hanging off them. He loved to share, with those who'd listen or wouldn't, that they were mystical symbols he'd seen while on ayahuasca.

"It was my biggest fear," Thomas said to Andrius and Emilija, "that the club would die without me."

It really was, though arguably he had much worse to worry about.

"But that you're carrying it on, I'm so pleased. So what did you get up to last Wednesday?"

"You ask like you haven't only been gone a few sessions."

Ah, fuck.

He spun around to see Greta, laughing nervously. Hair greasy as always. Inappropriately short shorts. Dirty sneakers. Crop top revealing her infected bellybutton piercing: swollen, reddish, tender, pained skin rejecting the metal bar. Not really in party gear. Just seemed out of place.

A new addition were the metal braces on her legs. He was sure she didn't need them but was determined not to ask. The one on her left knee browned and flaked at the hinges.

When and how had she slipped into the party anyway? And why had she shown up, just to antagonise him?

She poured herself a cup of the punch, her face contorting into an open-mouthed rictus, her gapped teeth making her appear more child-like than her age. Sixteen, maybe, unless older and held back a few school years.

Thomas pressed his lips together tightly as if to stifle his words. "Greta," he managed finally, "I haven't been to the club in half a year."

Her face became a mask of exaggerated shock. All knew she couldn't accept reality by now. And that you did *not* challenge her in *any* way.

"I'm leaving France tomorrow," Thomas added.

What did he have to lose? Looking upon her now, he saw only someone else's problem.

—

Thomas was the least Swiss Swiss person he knew of.

He couldn't vibe with his own people. He found them uptight, officious. They'd tap you on the shoulder if you were about to jaywalk. If passing through your neighbourhood, they might walk up your driveway and knock on your front door to inform you that you'd left your bins out for two days in a row. From across the street, if they spotted you smoking in a bus stop—even with no one else around—they might mime smoking then

15

wag a finger back and forth. *That's a no-no, Mr. Stranger!*

He found them insufferable. And they him.

For everyone's benefit, he fucked off to France, with the impossible aim of postponing life itself.

Across the country, he operated a slash-and-burn policy, spending a maximum of two semesters in a school as a foreign language teacher. He'd accept as few hours of these jobs as possible and move on before they became disenchanted with his poor performance.

The rest of his time he spent reading on park benches. Bukowski mostly. Sometimes other white men he considered the greats, his opinion of their mastery precisely coinciding with how little he understood what their books were about: Cormac McCarthy, Thomas Pynchon, the Jameses both Joyce and Franco. He'd read until homeless people bothered him for cash, interrupting his romantic idea of what his time abroad was supposed to look like.

He'd swan between bars at night, in his hippy attire, spouting his theories about how everyone was a secret hedonist and did only for themselves—a common young man's claim which said more about them than the world.

No matter. It worked.

Thomas slept with far more women than he deserved. No condoms unless they insisted, in which case he'd stealth them, peeling off the latex when he thought they wouldn't notice. If they did, on the way out he'd say they must have lost it up themselves.

Fake name, fake number, don't even live here, good luck with your life, honey!

In Zurich he'd smoked weed, chewed on mushrooms, and dropped acid. But he didn't have those connections in France and was too shy (lazy) to make new ones. So on most Friday evenings he'd pick up an armful of cheap wine bottles from the local supermarket, scurry back home, pull off his shirt and trousers, strip down to his boxers and hole up for the weekend. Suitably drunk, he'd binge indie movies in which white guys in plaid couldn't grow up. According to these films, this was okay. Thomas devoured them enviously, certain that any film he himself penned would be better. He enjoyed the feeling of this self-reassurance more than the satisfaction of writing something. Though he would pencil terrible and nonsensical imagery into the margins of his paperbacks, which often related to his last one-night stand.

The windows of her parent's house like haunted eyes opening upon the living room's mind-shelf.

She mounted me, the sky above her misted with skeletal leaves like the River Styx spied upside-down from Charon's boat.

Her breasts hanging like ripe melons dotted with blackberry nipples, sacs of ambrosia nuzzling my visage.

The bachelors in philosophy, which he left incomplete, worried away at the back of his head. But to return to the University of Zurich and finish his thesis was, to Thomas, the first step in growing up, which he had no intention of doing. Instead of memorising and interpreting the words of history's greatest, he dedicated brainpower to endless theories about how the way he lived was brave, actually. It was a finger up to 'suits,' capitalism, the mainstream—*and maybe Hollywood, somehow?*

He revelled in his supposed uniqueness. He and others of his ilk laid in wait to waste the best years of misguided young women who thought they could change them.

Like this he'd toured Marseille, Lyon, Nantes, Lille, Toulouse, and Strasbourg. Most recently, he'd landed in Rouen, to the northwest of Paris, to teach English and German at its *École des Langues et des Sciences Internationales.*

Now twenty-seven, he felt just as unready for the future as he ever had. The only change? Time had passed. If five years could zip by like that, with him feeling the same way about his preparedness—well then, so could every year.

But then he met someone who convinced him it was time for life's next steps.

—

It started with a student of his. On weekday mornings, you could spot her up the back of the school bus in a modest shapeless smock in some dark, neutral colour. By the time she arrived at school, she'd have thigh-high leather boots, a skirt that she'd rolled up around her waist, and a crop top which showed off her bellybutton piercing.

This was Zahra, Thomas' sixteen-year-old Iranian crush.

She sat up the front of his English classes, painting her nails, scrolling social media on the barely concealed phone in her lap, and constantly adjusting her top as if (Thomas erroneously believed) maximising his view of her cleavage.

By now, Thomas had proudly toured his John Thomas all over France, sleeping with women of every variety. He could write the Michelin Guide of Pussy and tick off every category. All but one.

Because this was the first time he'd ever wanted to fuck a student.

He did his best to concentrate in Zahra's classes, but considered himself powerless against her charms. And so he turned to the subreddits r/TeachBait, r/Educ8b8 and r/ApplesForTeach, whose explicit purpose was some variation on 'helping teachers not f*ck their students, no matter how sexy!'

I'm not gonna tell you where I am, Thomas would write, but age of consent here is fifteen. Secondly, I never claimed to possess professionalism. (I can only spell it thanks to autocorrect.)

Do I NoFap? AllFap?

Cold showers, hot showers?

What works for the rest of you?

I'm desperate and out of answers.

In theory, these forums were for consenting adults trying not to abuse certain power dynamics, though of course this became impossible to ensure. Their multifarious threads got flagged constantly. There were so many disturbing fantasies written there, clandestine photos of students posted with comments like 'Please help!,' 'Sweet Jesus what am I supposed to do?,' 'I can't hold it for much longer!'

And, well, worse.

So they got banned and deleted. Amazing they lasted any time at all. But the months of their existence were helpful for Thomas. He could commiserate and empathise with other teachers of endless varieties, positioned all over the globe, similarly possessed their inappropriate (at best) desires.

Thomas could have chased these communities through the darknet where they obviously scurried off to next. You could kill a subreddit, but the culture and the people who created it would persist. But instead, he needlessly lamented the loss of his outlet.

And he decided he had no other choice but to get

closer to Zahra.

—

Rouen, France!

Where in 1431 they burned Joan of Arc herself at the stake.

I wonder, did she know that I, Thomas Müller, would one day fuck my first student in that self-same place?

He booked an appointment with Mr. Dupont, whose dusty office was scattered with headmaster ephemera: binders of peeling, cracked plastic; warped, torn posters of Godard, Truffaut, Gerard Depardieu films from the nineties; an avocado pit skewered with wooden toothpicks, sitting in a stagnant glass of water on the windowsill. There was a rolodex on his desk. It must have been there since he started at the job. In the 'eighties?

"I want to start an after-school language club for kids who are fluent in a second language and want to learn a third," Thomas explained. "The languages they are fluent in, they teach to others. The languages they want to learn, they get feedback on from others."

"Sounds like a brilliant initiative, Thomas."

Mr. Dupont was a nervous man. White combover, the beginnings of jowls. He either couldn't grow a full moustache or shaved it at a weirdly close length so you could see right through it. Mustard-stained tweed sports coat over a pastel-blue shirt and tie.

"A brilliant opportunity for knowledge and

experience transfer," he continued.

I'm only interested in DNA transfer, Thomas thought.

"You know," Mr. Dupont added, leaning across his desk, "we're all really happy with how you're doing."

"Thank you," Thomas said, genuinely flattered. "I'm happy to be here."

What was he talking about? As far as Thomas could tell, he'd not given anyone any reason to praise him. And it wasn't like the man had visited Thomas' classes or anything.

This empty praise reassured him. Even the headmaster of a school was apparently too lazy to do his job properly. Maybe this meant Thomas wouldn't need to put as much effort into his future as he'd first thought.

Mr. Dupont cracked his knuckles, getting all serious. "You'll have to advertise the club on the school website, of course."

"Well I, uh—"

"It's a prerequisite of using school resources on extracurricular activities. But you'll want to, won't you? Best way to maximise membership." The spidery capillaries in his cheeks flushed with excitement.

No, Thomas did not want. Zahra would be his club's only member, if given the choice.

But to advertise was a small sacrifice. How many would voluntarily attend an after-school club anyway?

Mr. Dupont peeled a coffee-stained sticky note from a yellow stack by his laptop and wrote a reminder to upload some info for Thomas' club. The meeting having reached a natural end, he added, "You don't need such a strong reason to visit me, you know." He gestured to a broken wooden chess set on a nearby shelf. "We could play!"

"Oh wow," Thomas replied. "Thanks for the offer."

He shook the headmaster's hand, saddened at how easily the man believed him, and left.

—

Thomas brought up the club only once, in Zahra's English class.

"Oh, by the way," he took a stack of printed cards from his pocket, "I'm starting an after-school club." He passed the stack to Zahra for her to take one and pass on. "There's such a wealth of knowledge in this classroom alone. Just think what we could learn from one another!"

He could already tell who would show up based on how lonely they were. Andrius and Emilija, the Lithuanians. Rohit, Siddharth, and Avi, the Indian boys. Mikhail, the Russian.

"Like Zahra, for example!" Thomas gestured to her as if she had just occurred to him. "We could really use your expertise."

Zahra flicked her hair and eyed him up. "Why?"

"I assumed you spoke another language."

"Why?"

"You're Iranian, right?"

"Am I?"

"Aren't you?"

"Yeah, but I don't remember mentioning it in class."

"Okay." The fuck does that have to do anything? "And in Iran they speak...?"

She chewed her gum in thought, letting him trail off like she wanted everyone to notice he couldn't answer the question himself. "I mean, loads of languages. It's a bigger place than France after all." She rolled her eyes. "If you're asking me, I speak Persian."

Jesus Christ. Took her long enough.

"Well anyway," he said, clearing his throat, "you'd be a good fit if you wanted to come along."

"When is it?"

"Thursdays after school. It says so on the card."

"But like what time?"

"What time does school end?"

"Four p.m."

"That's when it is. It says so on the card."

"Until when?"

"It says so on the—five thirty."

"Huh." She examined his card. "I think I can make it."

He'd certainly taken on a challenge with her.

Thomas hated those.

—

Despite not giving a shit about his own club, Thomas was nervous before anyone showed up. He took a diffuser he'd brought in from home and put some drops of lemongrass oil in its reservoir. He fiddled with his laptop and the overhead projector, seeing if he could play YouTube videos at decent volume if things got too awkward. He made coloured paper chains and strung them around the room, just to do something with his hands.

Sure enough, the kids he'd already picked out filed into the annex just after four p.m. most Wednesdays. Andrius, Emilija, Mikhail, Rohit, Siddharth, and Avi— and Zahra too, when she could be bothered.

His idea was always to empower them to do their own thing. They loved this in theory, but rarely put it into practice.

"This could be a great resource!" Rohit once said. "Like, we could offer an amateur translation service. Maybe get money from some local institutions to do so?"

"What?" Thomas had been looking at his phone. This was on one of the days Zahra wasn't in attendance. "Oh. That's a great idea."

"So?"

"Go for it. You have my permission to apply to anyone you think might be interested."

The group would collectively frown at him, as if to

say, "No, that's not how it works. We dream shit up, you execute it." Crestfallen faces would follow as they realised, "Oh no, if I want things to happen, do *I* need to make them happen?"

This was healing for Thomas to witness. Who was he to blame them for their attitude? He'd acted this same way during group projects at university, thought of himself as the 'brains' or the 'creative engine' of the work, dreaming up stuff for others to do without making further contributions of his own. Those who displayed the most initiative, he reasoned they were just special, different from him. He'd delegate all his tasks to them and act stupid if they declined.

So Thomas agreed with his students: having to do stuff, if you wanted stuff to happen, was the worst. But as their teacher, it would be poor form to admit.

When Zahra did attend, she seemed to like the club the most. She'd sit with new members, explaining, "This is what we usually do at language club."

And Thomas would think, *Who the fuck is 'we?'*

He was glad she felt some ownership over this thing they had supposedly built together—but what did *they* do? He prepared all the activities. He found pop songs in their various languages and printed out the lyrics. He sourced interesting news articles about what was happening in their countries of origin. He illegally downloaded sketchy, dubbed versions of his favourite US comedies. He motivated them constantly despite their relentless complaints.

Most people, it turned out, would meet first to socialise and second do whatever a club was for. It could have been the Penguin Appreciation Society this whole time and it wouldn't have mattered. They just needed any excuse to hang out. They weren't folk who were confident enough to admit they enjoyed one another's company on its own merit, to meet for no particular reason. They needed some additional excuse, but had no intention of putting much work into whatever that excuse was.

Thomas would have thought this ideal before the club's foundation. His club, in so targeting these forlorn foreigners—the loneliest of the lonely, those most obviously discriminated against—meant that nobody around him possessed the wits or emotional intelligence to notice what he was really up to. And yet he'd come to care about all of them.

How can it be that people don't talk enough? Thomas wrote in the margins of Pynchon's Vineland.

People love to talk. Just not about important things often enough. Days slipping by in soul-silence. There are so many lonely people. You could fill your days trying to make them less lonely at the expense of yourself. At some point you just have to accept that the world is lonely and will be lonely your entire existence. You can't eradicate it in your lifetime. Barely know what to do with your own after all.

—

Greta showed up at the start of spring in skimpy clothing. A tank top and cut-off denim shorts with dirty sneakers. She held an elbow in her palm, head slumped over, and speed-walked to the back of the room.

Thomas waved an awkward hand at her, though she wasn't looking. "Hi?"

"Hi," she replied in almost a whisper, sitting down.

"I'm Mr. Müller."

She peered at him through her scraggly, dirty blonde hair. "Greta."

"Here for the language club?"

"Yep."

"How did you learn about us?"

"Internet."

"Greta…" Thomas paced around, considering his words carefully. "I've not seen you before. Whose class are you in?"

"Rousseau's."

Thomas turned to the clock behind him, then confirmed its time on his phone. "It's only three twenty. Shouldn't you be in his class now?"

"I'm not in it *yet*." She glared at him, her expression flipping with frightening rapidity. She dropped the intimidating look, twisting a tendril of hair nervously. "Or

I—I'm thinking about transferring here. To this school. So I thought I'd just show up and join your club."

Thomas folded his arms, thinking. The more fuss he caused about who could attend, the more attention he'd draw to the club and himself. The more formal it became, the less geared towards his agenda.

"That's okay, right?" Greta asked.

He shrugged. "I guess so."

And so Greta began as she planned to continue, by boxing Thomas into a corner until he had no option but to resignedly agree with her.

—

Thereafter, Greta shot down every activity Thomas proposed to the club.

He'd look at Zahra and say "How about a weekend trip to the cinema to see a foreign language film?"

"Good luck doing that here!" Greta would reply. "*No one* will take you up on that offer. While I still value the cinema experience, most other kids just stream shit for free on their phones."

"Instead of here in the annex," Thomas would suggest, "we could meet up at the German café one week—"

"You'd honestly take us *there*?" Greta would reply. "Come on. Their strudel is shit."

"We could all chip in and buy the same book in different languages," Thomas would start, "read it and then trade copies—"

"I find this offensive," Greta would interrupt. "There are a number of underprivileged kids in this school who would not like to reveal themselves by being asked for money they don't have."

She filled each response with her high-pitched, piercing laughter. It made Thomas shiver, like the sound of Styrofoam squeaking against itself.

"Uh, *no*," she'd say, interrupting Thomas on some other occasion to correct his advice in German to another student entirely. "We don't say it like that. I would have thought a *German language teacher* would know that!" Another jarring shriek of laughter.

"We say it in Switzerland," Thomas would reply calmly, trying to save face, move on, chalk up his mistakes to cultural differences.

"Do you?" She'd take out her phone and fact check him. Once she had some result, she'd stand up and march towards him, holding the proofs of his mistakes so close he could smell her body odor.

The first time she did this, he told her, "Greta, you're standing too close to me."

"No, I'm not," she'd whined.

"You're making me uncomfortable."

To this she'd gasped, looked around at her classmates, eyes flaring melodramatically.

She then headed to the back of the classroom and

burst into tears, sobbing the entire forty minutes that remained that session.

Thankfully, she did have some interest in writing to English-speaking penpals. Thomas attempted to elicit more information from her, but all she added was that "They're people who just need love. Their only flaw is that they went too long in life without it."

Thomas encouraged her to use club time on this activity alone. She'd hunch over her desk, eyes too close to the paper, talking to herself.

As relentlessly critical as she was of Thomas, Greta never presented her work to anyone else. She'd claim she wasn't ready and that they were ganging up on her. But it was clear to all that she was afraid of criticism.

So Thomas let her relentlessly fact check him. He let her stand too close and interrupt him, to burst proverbial water balloons over any of his suggestions. He came to consider it a backhanded compliment. Since she so rarely spoke, let alone with such candour, she evidently felt comfortable with him most of all.

—

Of all the girls she could have targeted, Greta became increasingly obsessed with Zahra.

She moved to the front of the room, beside Zahra, and began mirroring her clothing. Both had dressed skimpily, but Greta started to opt for darker colours until both were clad entirely in black. Greta painted her eyes with kohl and winged eyeliner. She dyed her hair with henna from dirty blonde to near-black. And Thomas' heart sank the day she came in hunched over with a patch over her bellybutton. Clearly she'd gotten it pierced just because Zahra had.

Her mimicry bordered on cultural appropriation. All were sure Greta herself would disapprove.

About as sure as they were that it wasn't worth pointing out.

She expressed a new-found interest in learning Farsi, presenting pages from her journal, which she'd translated, to Zahra.

Thomas considered this a positive sign. Zahra too, despite her probable dislike of Greta, was flattered at the opportunity to give feedback. But when she picked up on some minor issue of legibility, Greta crumbled once more.

She screamed, shot up from her chair, and marched to the back of the room. There she bawled for a constant half-hour while pulling out hairs from her crown.

Towards the end of this session, when all but Zahra had left—none of them asking Greta if she was okay, worried it would only extend her histrionics—Thomas held Zahra back.

He asked her, of Greta, "What do you think is up with that one?"

"She's having a tough time." Zahra nodded like a

concerned parent.

Drama was a sustenance that fed certain teenaged girls. It transcended language barriers, cultural boundaries.

"She's unlikeable because she's unlikeable." Thomas paced over to the primary-coloured kindergarten area in the far corner, his sandals squishing on its non-toxic foam tiles. "You can't extend leniency to everyone who's going through something. Someone always is, all the time. It's their burden. It sucks. But that's life." He examined the incomprehensible toddler scrawling sticky-tacked to the walls. "If I chose to act like Greta, you might examine my life with the same curiosity. Divorced parents. Mental health issues. Lonely in a foreign country—"

"Are you lonely?"

He turned to her. She looked concerned.

He paced back to her. "Point is, no sob story you could make of my life would excuse my bad behaviour. Don't you find it weird that Greta had no notion of coming to this school until our language club?"

Zahra placed her hands on her hips, drawing further attention to how skinny she was. "You should be proud!"

"Why?"

"You showed her there was something nice about this school. About our community."

Thomas undid the top button of his shirt. "I guess

so."

He looked out the window. Greta was outside, sitting between the double metal handrails on the school's front steps.

—

Thomas came outside and sat next to Greta on the handrails. One rail beneath their bums, arms flopping over the higher one. She was sniffling, still crying. She wiped her eyes.

It was warmer now, one of those rare spring days when the sun manages to break through. No rain, not yet, but dark clouds gathering in the distance.

"It's my family's fault," she said eventually. "They brought me to Rouen. They're super strict. They have all these high expectations of me. Not just of my academic performance but, like—I'm on a super restrictive diet because they want me to stay thin, find a man, and make them grandparents as soon as possible."

Thomas looked to the sky, the brightness paining his eyes. How did I get roped into this? I was just trying to get my dick wet before bouncing.

"What do *you* want?" he asked Greta.

"I don't know!" This set her off wailing again.

She composed herself faster this time. "You're the first person I've met here who actually smiled at me."

Thomas sighed. "Clearly you're going through a tough time and you have my sympathies. But perhaps it's best if you don't come to the club until you're in the right headspace for it?"

"Surely the fact that I keep showing up tells you I'm enjoying it?"

"Doesn't hurt to hear, too."

She just managed an ambiguous "Uh" in response, climbed off the railing and walked away.

"Greta, your—"

—

Thomas returned to his classroom. Zahra had left through some other exit in the building without saying bye, likely to avoid Greta.

Greta's school bag was up the back. A purple pastel-coloured rucksack with rainbow-coloured foam stickers of stars and unicorns on it.

Thomas unzipped it and pushed around the items inside.

Multiple pill bottles explained the death-rattle he always heard on her approach. The ones he recognised were painkillers, anti-depressants, anti-anxiety, laxatives. There was a bottle of ipccac syrup too, a vomit-inducing agent which, as far as Thomas knew, was these days considered too dangerous for personal use.

There was also a heavily folded and torn envelope, addressed most likely to one of Greta's 'penpals:'

Dallas 'Beau' Barrett

0067431P

TDCJ Polunsky Unit

3872 FM 350 South

Livingston, TX 77351

The door hinges creaked. Thomas tossed the letter back in the bag.

There was Greta. He picked her bag back up and held it out to her. Without a word, she marched towards him, snatched the bag, and left again.

Because she knew he'd looked through it?

Or because she was just like that?

—

On the bus home, Thomas looked up what he remembered of the envelope's address.

The Allan B. Polunsky Unit in Livingstone, Texas, was for male prisoners on death row. '0067431P' was the prisoner number for Beau Barrett, aka The Sunburst Killer. Ostensibly because he was a Texan, but it became associated with his alleged use of a shotgun to blow up the heads of young boys while raping them. Mr. Barrett had written an online manifesto which detailed the physiological and spiritual ways in which this mid-coital murder enhanced his orgasms.

Thomas recalled Greta's words about her penpals.

They just need love. They just went too long without it.

—

Thomas had predicted that Zahra would eventually turn against Greta—but not as quickly as she did.

Zahra visited him once during lunchtime, dressed in a black wool polo neck, black jeans, and white sneakers. Did this more conservative style mean her parents had rumbled her 'school bus makeovers?'

She turned to close his door.

This is it, isn't it? My seduction has worked! She's gonna fuck me right here!

"It's about Greta."

Ugh.

"I just need you to listen."

Ugh.

What followed was the cringe-inducing tale of Greta increasingly forcing her friendship upon Zahra during school hours. She probed her for fashion tips, asked for her favourite music so she could claim it as her own and found out who Zahra had a crush on.

"You, I told her. And that's why I'm here."

Oh, it is about me after all! She just had to find a roundabout way of telling me she liked me! Score!

Thomas grinned, folding one leg loosely over the other, like *Well well well!*

"She invited me up onto the roof after school last Friday," Zahra continued. "'The view is cool,' she told me. Took me to her favourite spot, led me there with my eyes closed, saying I had to trust her. But why would I? I opened my eyes when she was behind me and watched where she led me. It was the edge towards the school's trashcans down below. What was so cool about that?" Zahra paused to hold back tears before she carried on. "She whispered something—just to herself—but I swear it was 'He's mine.'" She shrugged, eyes going vacant. "Then she shoved me. Instinctively I grabbed her arm so she relented before pushing me with full force. Luckily she's so weak I managed to overpower her." She turned to Thomas again. "Don't you see? My crush on you set her off!"

I, uh—fuck.

Zahra stroked her arms, breathed deeper, more slowly. "She started laughing, like it was all a big joke. I clung to her, in hysterics. She laughed at me. 'You should see your face,' she said."

"Huh," Thomas said. "Maybe it was?"

Zahra frowned. "Maybe it was what? A *joke?*"

"You said yourself she needed extra attention."

Zahra scoffed. "And you didn't agree!"

"I'm allowed to change my opinion."

"Funny that your opinion always lines up with whatever requires you to do the least!"

He would make no effort to deny this. Even if it meant, as he was sure it did, there was now no way she would ever fuck him.

At that moment, Greta burst in, face bright red, her breathing exaggerated and shallow. It was like she'd been out in the corridor, listening while making herself look panicked, weak, and red-faced.

Zahra's eyes went wide. She huddled closer to Thomas.

He wrapped one arm around her. He only meant it protectively. All this chat of attempted murder was a real boner-killer after all.

"Whatever she's trying to tell you isn't true!" Greta screamed.

"Greta," Zahra said, "the police already warned you to stay away from me."

Greta ran to them and wrapped her arms around them both. Thomas held his head up, nose tilted away from her, irritated. Greta's standard BO combined with the clove cigarettes she'd started smoking to impress Zahra.

"It's just one big misunderstanding!" Greta wailed far too loudly given her proximity to the pair. "I would never hurt you, you're my best friend!"

"No, Greta, I'm not." Zahra leaned her head back and freed one arm to pat Greta on the back, while locking eyes with Thomas.

"Don't say that!" Greta, hysterical again, hugged them both tighter.

Zahra's lips twitched into an involuntary smile, like her brain had checked out. Like she had no idea how to handle this anymore.

Greta let them go with an almost violent shove. She pointed at Zahra. "We smoked weed up there. On the roof. She didn't want her parents to find out. So when Mr. Rousseau caught us up there and asked what we were doing, Zahra told him I'd brought her up there to kill her! Can you believe it?" Greta hugged Zahra, petting her hair like she was a fancy horse. "But I don't mind that you lied. We're still friends, right?"

"Greta, I can't be around you anymore."

Greta calmed herself, blood draining from her face almost instantly. "I understand."

"Everything will be okay," Thomas said to Greta. "You can go now."

She smiled, shrieked her awkward laugh, startling Thomas and Zahra both. "You're not gonna talk about me behind my back when I'm gone?"

"No." Thomas smiled, trying to match her energy, though her inappropriate levity creeped him out.

Greta strode from the room, vindicated, closing the door ever so gently behind her.

Zahra tutted. "*She* tries to push me off the fucking roof. *I* comfort her about how difficult that must have been for her!"

"Huh."

Zahra flicked him on the forehead. "That's all you have to say?"

"Were you smoking weed up there?"

"Is that at all the point anymore?"

Thomas bobbed his head around. "It's a pretty important detail." He tapped an index finger to his mouth in thought. "Which *you* left out."

Zahra threw her arms up in epic disappointment. "Oh, Mr. Fucking Detective." She gritted her teeth to stop from cursing him out further. "Yes, we were smoking weed. That's how she lured me up there!"

"And you didn't tell that to Mr. Rousseau."

"Who fucking cares?"

"Zahra!"

"I'm telling it to you now." Zahra's arms and hands shook, seemingly flailing of their own accord. "No, I didn't tell that to Mr. Rousseau."

"Look," Thomas said, "this is a private school and— I'll tell you this in confidence—her parents are paying for this."

"Shock fucking horror."

"They're pretty much indigent. But they prioritise her education, you know?"

"So do my parents. But they also prioritise my existence."

"Besides," Thomas said, continuing to ignore her, "the school year's almost over for me anyway, then I'll probably leave. So, what incentive do I have to do anything about this?"

"I—I can't believe you just said that out loud." Zahra took his hands in hers. "Mr. Müller, I'm telling you. She tried to kill me."

Thomas shrugged. "And she just told us she didn't."

She headed to the door. "Fuck you."

"Hey!" Thomas said.

"What?" She turned, wondering how on Earth he might defend himself.

"I know we got pally in this club of ours but I'm still your teacher. A little more respect, please."

"You're no longer anything to me." She looked him up and down, sadly. "You're—just another waster expat trying to coast on the mystique of having come from somewhere else. Shifting around once people get to know you better and discover it's the only thing about you that barely qualifies as interesting."

She left, slamming the door behind her.

The police concluded that, while it might be against school policy to allow pupils on its roof, it wasn't illegal for them to be up there. It *was* illegal, they added, to possess marijuana. But they found no evidence of that. They 'forgave' Zahra for wasting police time and advised her to find other ways of dealing with her friends.

Despite these monumental failings of anyone to give a shit, Zahra apparently tried one last time with Mr. Dunlop. Thomas learned this when Dunlop invited Thomas to his office to inform him, retelling Zahra's story in his own way, with the added detail that Zahra was transferring schools, for fear of her safety.

"Teenage girls, eh?" Dunlop concluded. "Who understands them?"

He wasn't telling this story because of any formal proceedings he wanted brought against Greta. He did so because Thomas knew both these pupils. He simply thought it an interesting anecdote. A nice excuse to get Thomas to meet him in his office for a chat.

—

After Zahra's departure, Greta was in something like good spirits.

She kept to herself at the back of the classroom during club events. She'd twitch, twist her hair and kick her feet, filled with nervous energy. She would smile and mutter to herself.

Thomas had been sat on the edge of his desk, like a 'cool teach,' rhapsodising about German and English swearwords, when Greta stood up, strode towards him, and slammed down a few crumpled handwritten sheets on his desk.

Thomas stopped talking, startled at the interruption. All heads turned in Greta's direction.

"I translated this from German to French and I want to know what you think of it."

"Sure, Greta."

She hovered by his desk. "Well?"

"You want me to read it right now?"

He looked around at the others, then back to Greta

"Okay, Greta." He sighed. " The rest of you—just keep chatting."

He turned his attention to the pages, getting them in order—there were numbers scrawled in the top corner—and began.

—

Timmy St Pork
by Greta Schröder

A suburban home.

Fat Fuck violently beats up Griselda, a German teenage girl.

Fat Fuck: I'm going to grab your cunt!

Griselda: Ow! You're a fucking psycho father I mean step-dad because you're not my actual dad! Get off me you fat fucking pig! How much pork have you eaten you stupid fat fuck? You disgust me more than the transgender people who perform brutal unnecessary surgeries on children!

A school.

Griselda meets Timmy St Pork, a language teacher. He radiates golden energy from his face!

Timmy: Hi, Griselda, it's nice to meet you! You're

my favourite!

Griselda: Wow, Timmy! You're my favourite right back!

Timmy is nothing but lovely to Griselda and he loves her and she loves him.

The suburban home.

Greta is in her mother and step-dad's bedroom. She smells something terrible, looks under the bed, removes a cardboard box, and opens it. Inside is her real dad's corpse, chopped up into bits.

Fat Fuck comes in.

Griselda: I knew it, you fucking fat fuck! You chopped up my real dad and hid him under the bed so you could fuck my mum over my real dad's rotting, diced up corpse! You really are a sick fuck!! A sick FAT fuck, that is!

A school.

Griselda comes to Timmy St Pork's after-school club to tell everyone about what happened to her real dad and ask for their help. The class is filled with jocks and cheerleaders.

Timmy: Griselda! You know you can't be here!

Griselda: Well, why the fuck not?

Timmy: Because all the other students will be jealous of how in love we are!

Griselda: Oh, right! Sorry everyone, I'll go!

She leaves.

In the corridor, a beautiful girl called Zeinolabedin, from the club, catches up with her.

Zeinolabedin: You should know, he said you're unlikeable because you're unlikeable.

Griselda: What a fuckhead!!

Zahra: I know, right?

Griselda: Thank you for telling me.

Zeinolabedin: Of course! What else are best friends for!

Griselda: That's right, we are best friends, aren't we!!

Zeinolabedin: YES!!!

Griselda storms out of the school.

The suburban home.

She takes a chainsaw out of her backpack and chops up her stepdad.

Griselda: Hahahahahaha!! Do you like that you fucking sick pedo psychopath?! I'm doing to you what you did to my dad! This is justice!!

The school again.

Griselda returns to the club and repeatedly stabs Thomas in front of everyone.

Griselda: (coated in Timmy's blood, addressing the rest of the club) It's so unfair that you got to be here and I didn't!! All you popular cool kids, you jocks and cheerleaders who don't understand how lovely some people are when you just make the tiniest fucking effort to know them!!

Everyone claps.

THE END.

—

Greta looked at Thomas, holding one arm. There was a giddiness about her. Like someone waiting to receive feedback on something of real value: somewhat sure she'd done a good job but still never certain whether her reader had enjoyed it.

Well, what Thomas thought of what he'd just read…

The 'jocks and cheerleaders' thing was a bit odd. The boys at this school mostly played hockey, rugby, or soccer. And there were no cheerleaders. It underscored Greta's removal from everyone else's world.

He was annoyed at himself for having confided in Zahra, given that she clearly repeated, word-for-word, what he'd said about Greta, directly to Greta.

Finally he noted Greta's lapses between the names she'd given her characters and the real people they were based on. It had been so obvious who she meant that this was barely worth mentioning.

"I'll be right back."

—

He waited outside the annex, having a smoke. Normally he didn't like the kids to see this. From his experience at other schools, they thought it gave them license to be rude at best, at worst to claim hypocrisy on the part of all teachers who wanted them to better themselves. "Got a light, Mr. Müller?" the biggest shits would sometimes ask.

But on this occasion he needed a smoke more than he cared about their opinions.

Greta's parents shuffled up the playground towards Thomas, looking older than he'd expected. Maybe in their late sixties, both of them. The dad wore a beige windbreaker and chinos. The mother drowned in an oversized, dowdy grey tunic, her hair in a Queen Elizabeth-esque bouffant. He wondered if they were grandparents pretending to be parents, because of some complicated family history.

He heard singing and turned to see Greta, dancing by herself up the hallway, unaware anything was wrong.

"Obsessed with you, is she?" the dad said.

"Wh—Why would you say that right away?" Thomas replied.

"It's what she does, pet," the mother replied, wringing her hands. "We've had to switch her out of schools a few times. It's gotten violent in the past."

Thomas ground his cigarette beneath his foot.

"Might either of you have—warned us about this before sending her here?"

"Well," the dad—*stepdad?*—said, "technically she sent herself here."

Thomas eyed up the dad. If he was the one from Greta's play, he wasn't fat at all. He was just a slightly older guy who took moderate care of himself.

"Whatever it was," Thomas said, "we probably would have needed more reassurance in the form of counselling hours and rehabilitation courses. You know—something!"

"We explained this to the *last* school?" The dad replied.

What fucking planet are these two from?

Mum placed an icy cold hand on Thomas' face. "Please don't put her through another change of schools. It will affect her mental health so badly. She has 'rejection sensitive dysphoria.'"

"Well, then", Thomas said. "She's really gonna hate what's coming."

—

"Is this because of my play?" Greta said.

Thomas had invited her to his office on Friday after school to break the news, following Gavin de Becker's advice in *The Gift of Fear.* De Becker recommended using a neutral room with no previous emotional associations, but Thomas didn't have use of anywhere

49

else. He'd at least managed to do it on a Friday after school, when everyone would be going home anyway, and long before she had any expectations of attending the next Wednesday club session.

Greta balled her hands into fists and squeezed them, groaning. "The thing I wrote, it was a work of fiction! How can you not understand that?"

"Greta." Thomas had to choose his words carefully. If she was intent on pretending it was fictional, there was no point in challenging her on its contents. "It's part of a pattern of inappropriate behaviour."

She huffed with exaggeration, her expression big and bug-eyed. She stamped around, folding and re-folding her arms against herself, jerking her head away from him as if to demonstrate her offence and her dismissal of him, over and over.

He'd pictured this often. Truthfully he'd wanted to do it the Wednesday a week and a half ago when he'd first read her play. Even having spent so long ruminating on how it might go, this was tougher, stranger—*realer* than he could have imagined.

"Okay." She grabbed her head as if thinking very hard. "So, I try to push Zahra off a roof and *that's* okay—"

"Are you admitting that now?"

"Allegedly, I mean, obviously!"

Mr. Dunlop, incidentally, had not been significantly disturbed by the play, on top of the roof incident, to expel

Greta. Thomas should have known that. The play was objectively less disturbing than the push—to people who weren't Thomas. But he'd ranted and filibustered at Mr. Dunlop regardless of how ineffective he knew it would be.

He also suspected there would be no further invites to chess.

"Greta, please lower your voice."

"I will not! I write a play you don't like and get kicked out of your club just because *you* have bad taste?" On the word "You" she marched forwards and started poking him, painfully, in the sternum.

He wheeled his chair away from her, only for her to reach forwards further to keep poking him. She was giggling. He had to grab her hand and bat it away from him, which made her gasp and clutch at it as if he'd hurt her.

She froze, her eyes going big and wide like a toddler who's just fallen off a chair. She was in that same brief moment of shock before the tears come. But soon she was wailing once again.

The emotions of teenagers were so wild. They had met much fewer people, and the intensity of their meagre years glared like the summer sun at its apex. They didn't see just how little something like this could matter in the scheme of things.

Regular teenagers, that is! And Greta's anything but

that!

As he watched Greta's histrionics, Thomas realised: It was Friday after school. Nothing stopped him from leaving to buy wine and start his weekend routine.

"There aren't even any fucking tears, Greta," he said, leaving her to her fake misery in his classroom.

—

Here he now was, celebrating his departure from Rouen with the kids who had come to matter to him most.

And Greta.

She rushed forwards and hooked an arm through his, sending a chill through him. "I'd really like to speak to you alone."

"Greta, this party is my last chance to see everyone. Can we do this afterwards?"

"I wouldn't ask unless it was urgent."

Everything was urgent with Greta. She was a constantly ringing alarm bell.

Impossible to ignore? No, to take seriously.

While on the surface it seemed she'd shown up to antagonise him, he also knew she wanted to express her appreciation of him. She just kept getting in her own way. Why not let her fumble an attempt at kindness one last time before he never saw her again?

"Fine."

She giggled like a little girl and ran towards some primary-coloured chairs in the kindergarten section.

She couldn't seem to figure out how to sit down, like she had trouble with her depth perception. Thomas held her wrists and lowered her into the seat.

"Thanks," she said. "I'm a little sedated."

On account of her leg braces? Some anger management regime?

Didn't seem to be anything wrong with her legs. Her inner elbows, on the other hand, were peppered with brutal-looking, bruise-coloured track marks.

Thomas should really say something. The primary emotion she evoked was pity. People like Greta—those so desperate, flailing, suffering, floundering, beating themselves up inside with the viciousness of a whole biker gang stomping on their own psyche—they had a way of drawing everyone into their rescue.

Even those who know it's up to us to save ourselves.

Greta tutted, sulking. "I'm only doing this because the other club members said I had to."

"Doing what?"

"Apologising to you."

"Is that what you're doing?"

She frowned. "Why didn't you tell me I had to?"

Thomas sipped his weak punch. "I didn't think negative feedback would improve—was worth my time." They hadn't even sprung for paper cups. They were those thin ribbed plastic ones dentists gave you to rinse your mouth out. "So, I just stepped away."

"But that's unfair!"

"Yeah."

"Ah, but it's so romantic, don't you think?" She linked an arm around his and leaned her greasy head against his bicep.

"I'm not sure I understand, Greta."

She turned to him and smiled. "How we shall die together!"

Thomas looked around the room. True enough, even in the time he spent looking at Greta, others had fallen to the floor, wheezing. The Lithuanian pair sat in two chairs by the wall, heads leaned together as if a couple in a long journey asleep in an airport. Except dead!

Mikhail the Russian slumped over his desk. Amazing to see such a big, muscular kid taken out by something so simple. A death that did not do him justice.

The three Indian kids were over by the window, in a corner, each of them vomiting. Maybe they'd be okay then.

Nearby all of them were emptied plastic cups of punch, fallen to the floor.

Mr. Dunlop dipped his head in to see what all the fuss was about. He yelped and ran around the room, shaking the students, trying to prop them in a way they could breathe or safely vomit. He took his phone out. He was calling for an ambulance.

Thomas began to feel nauseated, weak, sedated, his

vision narrowing.

The alarm that was Greta, she had kept on blaring at the same volume it had since he first met her.

You become deaf to it. You can't hear when it requires real attention.

Or perhaps it did from the very first time I met her.

"Did you do something to Zahra?" he asked.

"I *forbid* her from being here."

Heavy implications in that 'forbid.' Of a violent death elsewhere. If this was the end of Greta, she'd probably ended her parents, too. Just like in her terrible play.

Greta was sliding to the floor in her chair.

"Punch didn't even taste good," Thomas said, chuckling.

All he'd done for five years at various other posts—chopping and changing before they had time to notice he wasn't doing a great job, off to disappoint someone else—was the bare minimum.

The one time he'd wanted to make an impression, to be somehow special to his pupils—that was what ended his life.

There they were, Greta and Thomas. Two self-involved outsiders. Two creepy manipulators. Two terrible writers. Heads pressed against one another, dying together.

Greta was in tears, her voice going high-pitched and

whining: "Are you mad at me?"

Thomas had plenty of reason if he wanted. She'd made his biggest fear—that the club would die without him—come true.

Well, almost. Turned out it would die *with* him.

But didn't he also have Greta to credit for his last-minute growth?

She showed him that whether you had children, or believed in marriage, or wanted a nine-to-five, or busked and hitchhiked your way across the country until you forgot your own birthday—there was no ideal, simple life in which you evaded all responsibility. No place on Earth you could hide out where others wouldn't organically fall under your care.

So, he said, "No, Greta. 'Mad' isn't the word I would use."

THE MOTH & FLAME

"The title." Oliver Baring swirled his wine around before downing the full glass of it. "It just means 'Goodbye, Sadness.' So, call it that!" He shook his head. "These pretentious young twerps, I swear."

Ben leaned his elbows on the table. "Sometimes a foreign language title can be cool." Recalling that 'elbows on table' was poor restaurant decorum, he quickly returned his hands to his lap.

"You'd hate the writer too, Son. What little I've ever managed to see of him—not a big fan of people, as if anyone is!—has left much to the imagination. Random loner who barely ever leaves the house. Wouldn't know a crime if it burst in his bedroom and bit him on the ass."

Ben flicked an earlobe nervously. "When I, uh, asked if you'd read a good script lately, Dad, I was—referring to my own."

"What? Oh. Course I read your script." Dad smiled, teeth already stained by red wine. "And my first impression"—obligatory nervous laughter—"is that it's long." He ran his tongue over his teeth, clearing them of steak bits. "I like to number scenes. Do you know how many there are in your script?"

Ben spooned up his rice. It was fluffy, rich with coconut flavor, candied almost. "You're about to tell me, though I'm not sure why."

"A hundred and thirteen." Dad laughed, mouth full of steak once more.

Ben's eyes rested on Dad's dish. Medium rare, perfect juiciness. And he could almost taste the Béarnaise sauce's creaminess.

Wouldn't ask Dad to switch. Didn't want Dad to have the satisfaction of knowing Son wanted to. Everything a power play to London Dad.

Ben slathered his swordfish in mango salsa. So sweet and tangy, he could forget it was fish at all.

"What did you think about the content?" Ben asked. "Of the script."

"Hm?" Dad seemed to have spotted someone more important. He looked back at Ben. "Still mulling it over."

You could pass Oliver Baring a script and he'd comment on it like he knew what he was talking about— but Ben wasn't sure what his dad actually did. Dad's latest position was as Red Bus Films' 'talent advisor.' Sounded like it had something to do with funding films and finding new up-and-coming folk. He frequently appeared at various schmoozey events, went out to lunches with fancy people and appeared in their social media photos, like he was someone worth knowing. He was an invited speaker, a TEDx talker, a special chair.

Yet if you asked him to describe his duties, out came word salad. Plus he'd had no new IMDb credits in years, except 'special thanks' for some random indie videogame sequel, which Ben assumed was a mistake Dad hadn't bothered to correct yet.

"Son." Dad gestured wildly with his glass, red wine sloshing dangerously close to the rim. "Listen to me. Film isn't as magical as it looks from the outside. You got that job lined up at that place, stick to that." The job was in Leatherhead with MembraneSoft, a company that supplied industrial gases for steelmaking. Hardly competition for licking 'disco paste' off a model's ass in the back of a sports car.

"You don't want to be like me," Dad continued. "Up late at night, wondering where the money's coming from."

Ben nodded, slicing his swordfish with the steak knife. He'd run out of salsa, the fish alone tasting metallic and too salty, though mercifully weak in its fishiness.

Once they'd eaten, they had nothing to do but talk to one another again. Dad, blotting Béarnaise off his lips, broke the uncomfortable silence first: "I'm sure you don't believe the rumors."

Ben had decided he'd let Dad bring it up or leave it unspoken. "Why would you be sure of that?"

Luis kindly interrupted, bringing the drinks to accompany their upcoming desserts.

"You're Oliver Baring, right?" Luis held his palms up to indicate the dicey nature of what he was about to suggest.

Ben winced at Luis. Wherever he was going with this, it was not good. But it was bound to entertain him nonetheless.

"It's just—I'm such a huge fan of Red Bus Films!"

Ben saw his dad's shoulders fall. Evidently, he'd relaxed.

"Well, thank you," Oliver said.

"I actually came here to get into the film business myself," Luis said.

Ah, fuck. Here it comes.

Ben was familiar with interruptions of this variety. Shit was about to get cringe.

"In fact," Luis continued, "I got bored of getting offered so few interesting roles, and seeing so many bad films produced, that I had a go at writing my own."

Dad groaned audibly in frustration. Only because he knew, as Ben did, that there was no stopping someone when they got like this. You just had to get through it.

"Now," Luis said, "I won't take up too much of your time, but it basically goes like this."

BIG DEATH

Filip came home to find Kristine pushing a book into their indoor fireplace with a poker. Flames ate the pages, turning them as they lost their weight and became ash.

When a corner of black card fell onto the carpet, he ran to stamp out its embers. On the card were hearts drawn in sparkly gel pen. It came from a photo album.

The fire crackled and Kristine shuffled back as green flames sparked with a pop! "One of the USBs," she croaked. She was in her gray sweatpants as always, black hair tied back, fringe growing over her eyes.

"What did you—"

He looked around the apartment. The walls were bare, save for corners of tape with remnants of torn photos stuck to them. Along the windowsills, the photo frames lay face down. In the kitchen area, plain circular magnets on the fridge pinned nothing at all.

"No!" He took out his phone and scrolled through his gallery of photos and videos. She'd deleted everything that synced with the cloud.

He grabbed at her frail wrist, wrenching the poker from her. She cowered beneath him and scurried over to the couch, where she tugged at a thick-knit blanket, pulling it around her. An amateurish pastel-pink thing, one of her many anxiety-staving crafts.

His body released of tension and he placed the poker by the furnace. "Have you eaten?"

"Why is that always your go-to?"

"It couldn't hurt." He turned and met her dead eyes. "Because I don't know what I'm doing. Did you talk to Dr. Ramberg today?"

She shook her head. "The free trial ended, so I deleted her."

"I said I'd pay."

"She isn't working. Nothing is."

He went to her and pulled the blanket tightly around her. "Let's get you a cup of tea and then go for a walk."

She glanced to the window behind her. "Oslo doesn't know that it's spring yet. The snow never lets up."

It piled in thick layers on the sidewalks down below, footprints mashing it into slush on grit laid just about anywhere. Streams of dirty water flowed through gutters that had spent the winter months constantly gurgling.

He stretched his neck. "Another afternoon of video games, then."

She nodded. "That I can do."

In the kitchen, he turned the kettle on, using its loud boiling to disguise the raggedness of his breathing. This was critical. All those memories burned and trashed—it was her biggest step yet in the project that she had obsessed over for months now: erasing herself.

It was probably enough to get her sectioned, if he wanted to pursue that. But would that really help? Wouldn't that mean he had failed? Because if not him, who else did she have?

He took her a cup of tea in a pink mug, cradling his hands over hers and feeling her warmth return.

"All better now," she said, her voice devoid of emotion. "Can you promise me something?"

"Let me hear it first."

"Don't keep anything of mine when I'm gone."

He gripped her around the shoulders, almost spilling her tea. "You're not going anywhere."

She grabbed his arm and leaned her head against him. "It's important. You can't bring other girls back here with pictures of me on the mantle."

"Hey, look at me?" He let her go and sat cross-legged on the carpet before her. He tapped his head. "There isn't a world in here without you in it."

She looked back to the tea, blowing on its surface. "Well, start making one."

—

"So, we finally meet."

Marina smirked at Filip. She lifted the mercury breeze from the round metal table between them and took a sip. She had straightened black hair, dark eyes and wore a liquorice red leather jacket, with lips and nails to match.

"Did Nils tell you about me?" Filip asked. He looked

away from her face as if she shone with bright light. Eventually his eyes rested on the tattoos of interlinking black hexagons that swarmed up her forearms. "What did he say?"

She rolled her shoulders, her jacket crinkling. "Nils said you were sweet and that we were a good match. So much so that he would bravely give me."

Filip dared a look at her face. "Well, he has no shortage of backup ladies."

"I figured as much." She smiled kindly, tilting her head.

Filip's hands started shaking. He tried to grip the table to steady himself, but it was part of the simulation. The ambient noise of conversation from surrounding tables murmured in his ears, but when he looked around, he couldn't see anyone.

"First time using a headset?" she asked.

He grinned. "No. First time for this, though." He dried his hands on his sweatpants. "Sorry I'm not more presentable. I—hadn't planned on this when I came here."

She frowned. "Huh? Oh, what you're wearing. But I just see your head on a tux, seriously."

"Oh. Good, I guess?"

She reached a hand out to his, her fingertips dissolving where they met his skin. "You'll get used to this. Hey, at least you know your date won't walk out on you or throw their drink in your face."

"Is that what you want to do?"

"To you? No." She leaned forward, her elbow glitching into the table. "We don't have long left. Anything you want to ask me?"

"I don't know what's allowed."

She sighed. "I can take the lead. So, last year I got a job here in Oslo and came over from Tbilisi in Georgia, where I'm from."

"Oh." Filip picked at his fingernails. "Then why did—"

Her image flickered and disappeared. Psychome's smiling cartoon brain mascot took her place, along with the message, *Thanks for stopping by!*

He took off the headset. Around him, old bleak strip lights glowed through the dusty air, the night's stars shone through perforations in the roof and warm drips of condensation fell from bare air conditioning pipes, their worn insulation peeling away. Hundreds of old and rusty bar stools populated the room, around half in use by customers who mostly slouched upon them. *Åndbaren* hangar's more experienced gentlemen balanced their headsets' weight while engaged in conversation.

Filip went up to the bar, returning the headset to Nils, a large ginger-bearded guy with dark moody eyes, squeezed into an ill-fitting black sweater with *Åndbaren* embroidered over the pocket.

"So, how did you like Marina?" Nils beeped the headset against a computer on the plastic counter, his face glowing with the expectation of salacious details.

Filip smiled. "How much was I supposed to get from a minute's chat?"

Nils placed his hands proudly on his hips. "As we like to say here at *Åndbaren*, the Tantalizing Freebie option is long enough for you to fall in love at first sight." He leaned over the bar, fingers splayed through his beard. "Did it work?"

Filip shrugged.

Nils lifted a panel in the counter and gestured for Filip to join him behind the bar. He filled two glasses with beer from a tap.

Filip took one of the beers and sniffed at it, rotating the glass in his nervous hands. "I can't believe you manage this place by yourself, it's huge."

"Crazy, right? But thanks for coming. The company thinks better of me the more people I get to check this place out." He looked across the hangar, where rows of mostly men faded off into the distance. "Every patron counts." His sweater rode up over his belly as he sat down. He tugged awkwardly at it. "I'm uh, not in the good books since they 'reassigned' me here."

"When I first came in, I wondered why the place didn't turn off the clientele. Then I saw the head gear." Filip looked at the boxing headsets. Green lights on their sides waved like glow sticks at a concert. Nearby, a scruffy ginger-haired kid held his arms out and tongue-kissed the air. "And the smell of mold fades soon enough," he added.

Nils held out a hand. "Well, yeah, the tech distracts anyone from anywhere. I swear, if I worked outside this building, I'd superglue it to my face."

"You're hooked, huh?"

Nils took a swig of beer then licked at his foam moustache with limited success. "I'm a total ghost player. Different woman every night. They're always so grateful for my company. I mean, without me, they don't exist."

"So, who's Marina? Why would she sign up for this?"

"It's a way of living on." Nils looked back across the room, half-dreaming.

"But why live on in a dating game?"

"It's no game." Nils pulled his arms and cracked his back. "There are other uses for ghosts in development of course, as rich and disturbing as the imagination allows. But since Psychome's survey data shows that dating is the most popular application of their tech, it reached beta testing first. The ghosts—yeah okay, they usually signed up for the money. There's a big cash incentive. If not that, they're usually trying to live out a fantasy of their own in the 'afterlife.' Which isn't allowed. You find those ones out soon enough because they lie about their age. It gets them suspended. Authenticity is what attracts patrons to ghost dating."

Filip gritted his teeth as if to stifle his next question, but blurted it anyway. "So, Marina was really alive once? Not just a simulation?"

Nils scoffed. "That's why she costs so much to be with."

"How do we know she's, uh, gone?"

Nils glanced around before speaking. "Look, if she wasn't dead before they extracted her ghost, she sure was afterwards. They can't do it otherwise, as far as I know. Last time I checked, all I found were experiments they did on pigs like a decade ago. In one step, they replace the brain's blood with embalming fluid. So, like, there's no way to do that while keeping the pig alive." He lowered his head, looking around. "I've got vids of it if you wanna—"

He stopped himself as a female-presenting customer stood by a computer at the end of the bar. Tanned and frail, she held out her headset with trembling fingers. Nils went over to her, beeped the headset against the computer's side and thanked her for coming.

He removed a chip from the headset and showed it to Filip. "None of my girls are allowed in the cloud, see. If this bar is a success, they'll be Psychome's lifeblood one day."

Filip grimaced.

Nils crouched beneath the counter. In front of him were various steel lockers of different dimensions with keypads and locks on their front. "Why did you come here if it's so creepy?" He beeped a code into one of the lockers, opening it and placing the chip on a tray inside before closing it again.

"I wanted to meet you in person."

Nils stood back up and leant on the bar. "If you say so."

"Look, I—" Filip tugged his jacket tighter over his frame, feeling a chill. "I don't want to get into it, but I'm not ready to date yet. I thought this might be a—stepping stone. Or something."

"And?"

"I'm afraid I'll hurt you if I say anything more."

"Right. Let's leave it, uh? Wanna hang out in the back and have a Hammerdrive sesh?"

Filip placed his beer on the counter, having barely touched it. "Not in the mood."

Nils stood up straight and gestured towards Filip. "Fil, we've played it together for like fourteen hours straight. More than once. You test videogames for a living!"

"Yeah." Filip touched his cheek, his face flushed with warmth from his encounter with Marina. "It feels like work sometimes."

—

Filip took the magnotram in the direction of Oslo Sentrum. On the journey, a lab coat-clad hologram of Psychome's CEO, Dr. Åste Magnusson, thanked him for today's visit to their test facility. Her ponytail bobbed with ebullience as she asked if he would answer a few follow-up questions. Instead, Filip put in his earbuds and looked out the window.

Fjords, lined with firs both real and artificial, passed by. Neon streamed along the big paths, emanating from the electric blades of late-night street skiers.

The tram hacked Filip's earbuds and told him to listen to Magnusson or pay for a ticket. He consented to pay.

He soon reached his cramped apartment in a high-rise just east of the city center. Once in the front door, he headed to the kitchen and made an open salami and cheese sandwich on stale bread. He took this to the racing chair in front of his wall-sized TV screen. Along the bottom was a steel drawer, from which he pulled out a wireless wheel.

He pressed the wheel's home key. The screen blasted him with light and steel pedals slid out their slots in the floor. *Buzz.* A hologram of his kart appeared around him. He had arrived on Supertrak's Intergalactic Circuit.

Lights counted down: three, two, one. The engine revved and his kart sped down the gleaming metal track against an artificial night sky, blooming with colorful constellations. The floor tilted with him as he drove, the chair vibrating as he bashed off that initial tight corner as usual. He accelerated into the first loop, which took him up through the stars. As the metal kart track before him dissolved into clear diamond, he floated, alone, free.

Zoom.

The fastest speed run always overtook him after this. She roared ahead in her tricked-out bike. She'd designed it to look like an old Harley, but it hovered on levitating superconductor pads. He focused as they both entered a twisting ribbon of track, seasickness swelling in his stomach. The kart ran over silvery speed boots and deftly avoided spikes strewn across his path.

They entered a long straight together, he and the ghost kart. The course was nearly over. With his better acceleration, he had the advantage.

The finish line approached. His front wheels aligned with her bumper. He gained on her, close enough now to read the name that hovered above her head: *Keeks*.

He hit the brakes.

"Loooooossseerrr!" she cried at him as she sped across the finish line, taking first place for perhaps the thousandth time.

Because if Filip beat the 'ghost,' it would disappear forever.

It wasn't a ghost like they had at *Åndbaren*, of course. It was just a kart, some lap times and that one sound clip that said "Loser!"

At least it would seem that way to anyone but Filip

"I told you," he said to the screen. "Can't think of anything better than wasting my evenings with you." He dropped the wheel in his lap. "You'd hate that if you knew."

—

Over the weeks that followed, Filip would return to *Åndbaren*. As he did, Marina became as real to him as anyone else.

She told him about the meat dumplings her mother used to make, how she'd dip them in mayonnaise and vinegar. The idea made Filip shudder, and she laughed.

He explained his job, how he walked around in simulations all day until reality stopped meaning anything.

"At least you get to leave the simulation at four p.m.," she retorted.

She regaled him with a description of her walks to school as a teenager, how frost clung to her eyelashes.

"That happens to me too!" he said. "During the winters in Oslo."

He thought of Kristine's frozen face, how she'd giggle when showing off her white eyebrows.

One time, he worked late and missed his appointment with Marina. The following week, when he managed to return to her, he abstained from apologizing until he'd gauged her reaction—which was nothing at all. She didn't know. So, he went on to tell her about his parents' cabin, how he loved to leave the city and spend a weekend cross-country skiing.

"I'd love to join you next time," she replied.

The notion filled his chest with warmth, even as he wondered if it was just part of the fantasy he had paid for, or a real possibility. Not an inventor himself, he couldn't imagine what they'd let the ghosts do after this test phase. Maybe they'd let him 'keep' her. With her permission of course.

With time, they relaxed into the dance around the one thing they couldn't talk about, focusing instead on the relationship they'd have one day.

"A long, long-distance relationship," Marina quipped, winking.

—

"Hey, get off me, man. I'll ban you if I have to!"

That was Nils, shouting at a customer over by the bar.

When Filip's session had ended, he took off his headset and approached. The customer had deeply ingrained lines in his cheeks and looked like he was trying to assault Nils with just a glance. As Filip got closer, he smelled stale cigar smoke. He mouthed to Nils, *You okay?*

Nils kept his focus on the customer but shook his head. This wasn't the time to talk.

Filip retreated to a bar stool near the door and waited

as the men talked further, out of earshot. He watched as Nils flailed his arms and stabbed at the air with an index finger.

Eventually the customer turned and headed to the front door. As he passed Filip, he said, "The staff here are very rude."

Filip walked back to his friend, letting Nils initiate the chat with whatever info he was willing to provide.

Nils pinched at the bridge of his nose as if suffering from a sudden headache.

"Dude, he—" He slapped his forehead. "When he gave the headset back, I complimented him on his choice of lady. Because I—used to date her."

Filip snorted. "Ouch. Say no more."

"You inspired me by the way!" Nils clapped his hands together.

"Oh yeah?" Filip sat back down, rubbing his eyes. A mild silhouette of Marina had burned into his retina in blue and took a while to fade.

"I've been seeing this one ghost, Laila. She's a handful, but I'm sticking with her. I haven't loaded any others in days. Aren't you proud?" Nils raised an eyebrow. "Dude, you look awful."

"Is this what Marina does to her customers?" Filip's voice was a fragile croak.

Nils leaned in. "Because we go way back, and you encouraged me when I got this job—well, I reserved her for you. Some others have tried to book her through the site, but I cancelled their appointments and cited technical difficulties." He squared his shoulders. "They went with other ghosts and that was that. I haven't raised suspicion yet. Don't know how, though. What do they think is up with her?"

Filip recoiled. "You don't have to do that."

"Fine."

"But—can I talk to her a bit longer?"

Nils walked over to the computer, scanned the headset against a reader and gave it back to Filip.

Filip wore it with the visor over his forehead as he made his way to an empty table.

Beside him was that scruffy ginger kid who kept kissing the air. He was in the same jeans and polo as before. Did he ever leave?

Filip shook his head and lowered the visor over his eyes.

"Good to see you again, Fil," Marina said as she apparated opposite him at the table. "It's been too long."

She wore a sparkly black dress. A matching cardigan draped on the chair behind her. She cradled an enameled mug of tea and blew at its vapor.

He swiped at the mug, his hand going straight through it.

She frowned, sat up stiffly and shooed the mug away like smoke, its image dissipating at the touch. "I'm just trying to make this seem normal."

"But it isn't. At all." He clenched his hands into fists. "So, what happened to you?"

"Well, that's direct." She bit her lip. "Everyone has a past, but only you can have a future with me."

"You tell all your clients that?"

She rolled her tongue across her teeth, not breaking eye contact as she considered what to say next. "I, uh—did it to myself."

"You—" Filip held his breath, rendered speechless.

"You did ask."

"I know, it's just—you're not the first person I've—lost, in that way."

She held up a finger. "You didn't really 'lose' me though."

"Didn't I?" He motioned for her to lower her hand. "My other friend—she didn't sign up to donate anything. She acted like there wasn't a useful cell in her body. If you're telling the truth, why would you want to be any type of ghost, let alone one that dates?"

Her stoic expression faltered. She rolled her eyes. "Oh, what good does it do to talk about it now? You can't bring me back." She gestured to herself. "This is all that's left. The least we could do is enjoy it."

"I don't believe you!"

Filip felt his neck jerk around. It was Nils, wrenching the headset from him. Once it was off, his friend looked at him with concern.

Customers from adjacent tables, from as far as five rows away, turned to look at Filip. The headsets strapped across their foreheads shimmered like bluebottles' eyes. He must've been louder than he realized. Even that lonely ginger teenager from before observed Filip with unwarranted pity.

Nils took Filip by the wrist and dragged him back to the bar. "Let's get you a glass of water, uh?"

Filip frowned at the ginger kid, forcing him to break eye contact. "What right does that one have to judge me?"

Nils tutted. "Oh, he's nice, really. His boyfriend died in a speedboarding accident. He comes here to visit him. He's actually why I convinced Psychome to introduce a loyalty bonus. There's no other way he could afford to stay here as long as he does."

Half the clientele re-engaged their virtual fantasies and paid Filip no mind. Some looked at him as if they too were due some life re-evaluations.

Filip made to leave but turned back to Nils. "You used to work at Psychome HQ."

Nils clenched his teeth and muttered, "I told you that in confidence." He pressed his fingertips to his jaw, relaxing the muscles, and sighed. "You know what? Sure. I blagged my way into a job I didn't have the experience for, thinking I could learn it on the go. Not only did I underperform but I failed two"—he held up a peace sign for emphasis—"random drug tests. So they 'reassigned' me here." He stuck out his tongue. "What are you gonna do about it?"

"You still have your pass, for the building?"

"What, you don't believe they even considered me for a better position than this?" Nils reached behind the bar to one of the metal safes, unlocking it and pulling out a tray. He held it out to Filip. In it were a collection of broken ghost chips and an old plastic Psychome ID card, battered and browning.

Filip snatched the card and bolted to the exit.

"Hey! You won't find out anything about her there! And you can't just—"

—

Psychome's headquarters, a glass bullet of a building, turned the spring sunlight into big golden pixels with its many square windows.

Filip shielded his eyes as he looked up.

Hiss!

He jumped with fright. On either side of the white flagstone path before him, stalk-like jets fired out the grass and spritzed the surrounding park with synthetic scents of nature. Pine, elderberry, the earth after rainfall. The smells chemically calmed him. He wondered if there were other substances mixed into the spray.

He ventured through the park, across the path, into the HQ building.

Inside, he took Nils' card from his pocket, surreptitiously examining the photo. Nils was thinner then, closer in appearance to Filip now. With any luck they had this old image in their system. He kept his pace, trying not to look suspicious, as he traversed the vast lobby, one wall of which was a large mirror of smoky glass. Behind there were surely a set of security guards.

When he reached the entrance turnstile, he pressed the card on its reader, wincing. To his surprise, it beeped and a green light appeared. He walked through, scurrying quickly round a half-wall and looking for security cameras out the corner of his eye.

Three young women in pencil skirts walked by, their voices fluttering through the corridor.

He headed up a spiral staircase to the top floor, in search of a free office within Nils' region of security clearance. In a glass-walled quad below sat a self-sustaining atrium of palm trees, orchids, and passionflowers. Vines and ivy snaked across its glass walls like big green veins. He passed above it, across the upper floors' wire-suspended walkway, through the atrium's humid air and beams of sunlight from the mountain-shaped glass roof above him.

On the walkway's other side, walls of photoreactive glass darkened to show which offices were occupied. Filip dodged white-smocked staff members on his way and ducked into a vacant room.

Inside were workstations with computers, beneath a wide window that showed the vast gardens down below. Outside, flying silver spheres buzzed lazily around, misting the immaculately mowed lawns.

Filip went up to one of the stations, clearing sticky notes and paper coffee cups out the way. There was a slot on the computer for a building pass. He inserted Nils' pass, the computer switched on and he searched for Marina.

An overexposed passport photo of her looked back at him.

Age: 24. 5' 6". Female.

Under attachments, there was a single text file with a few uneven strings of numbers in it. He took out his phone and snapped a pic of them.

"So you're looking for Marina, Fil."

Filip swiveled around on his chair in shock. By the door, Dr. Åste Magnusson's semi-transparent head stared him down. A hologram. Behind the head was a security guard, a lady with her blond hair tied in the same ponytail as Magnusson's. In one of the guard's hands was a plastic disc from which Magnusson's head emerged.

Filip jerked back as the guard tossed the disc in his direction. Magnusson's full body rose up from the floor, in its white lab coat, suit trousers and turtleneck.

Filip's eyes widened, but he remained silent.

"Surprised to see me like this?"

He shook his head. "Busy woman like you can't be everywhere at once."

"Incorrect."

Filip wheeled the office chair a little closer. "Are you a ghost?"

She shook a finger. "We don't use the 'G' word. You'd know that and more if you ever listened to my story on your tram home from *Åndbaren*."

He pressed a cold hand to his cheek, his face flushing red.

This evidently delighted Magnusson. "Have you heard of Huntington's disease?" She crossed her arms.

Filip leaned back. "Can't say that I have."

"It's a type of dementia. And I've got it." She frowned. "Or I had it. My body did, I mean. You'd think I'd have a logical way of saying that by now." She clasped her hands behind her, stretching her back. "There's still no cure. So, after I tested positive for the disease, I worked even harder to develop our brain-downloading tech. I jumped ship to this form before I even exhibited symptoms." She paused as if for congratulations.

Filip scratched at his chin. "Interesting. What does 'jumping ship' entail?"

"Becoming a medical marvel, a pioneering scientist. Getting to work well into middle age and beyond." She examined her nails. "It does not entail losing brain functionality or crapping my pants. A huge plus, you'd agree." She rolled her shoulders then looked back at him. "Difficult prognoses aside, I'm sure everyone will want to sign up when we go full scale. Such a relief to shuffle off the mortal coil of one's own volition. You should try it sometime."

He looked to the table behind him. "You can't do this, though." He knocked some paper cups to the floor.

Magnusson's guard approached him with menace, but Magnusson held out a hand to stop her. The guard looked to Filip with a pleasurable gloat in her expression.

"I'll be a robot soon," Magnusson said. "Maybe even a whole fleet of them. Then who's laughing?" She approached him, playing with a name tag on her coat pocket with a look of dismay. "Marina is here."

Filip's head jerked with surprise. He tried to disguise it as a neck stretch.

"Not in the building, I mean." She leaned forward and tapped through Filip's skull. "In here."

He leaned back to remove the finger, sinking into the chair's memory foam. He looked Magnusson up and down with confusion.

"The first time you spoke to Marina," Magnusson said, "what did she order?"

"I—I think it was a mercury breeze."

"Kristine's drink."

He gritted his teeth.

The silent guard looked at him with docile, unthreatened eyes.

"You had to want to care for Marina. Choice of drinks is the first and most common trigger. Maybe it was the way she flicked the black braid of her hair, certain patterns in her speech. I'm sure you could name more." Magnusson's eye seemed metallic in the office's shade as she moved to the window. "During your last session, for example. How did she say she died?"

"You're spying on me."

"Not me, no." Her voice turned hollow. "He's a bit of a slacker, but he plays the part of casual gamer buddy so well. You'd attest to that, I'm sure. As would his other marks. If only they knew." She held a hand out to Filip, palm up. "He invites you to the bar to 'try out some new tech.' Your brain does all the work after that. You created Marina in your own vision."

Filip held back tears. "To what end?"

"To help you heal." She looked out the window to the lawn and the misting metal spheres. "A blind study. Simulations assisting the bereaved. Clever, no? You would've affected our results had you known. But your contribution will help so many."

"You think you can just—"

The guard looked at him sternly.

Magnusson turned and dragged a finger across her lips in thought. "I must advise against the legal action you're considering. Let's not waste each other's time. Now, we've held onto Marina's memory as it built over your last twenty sessions. But we have no further need of it."

The guard unclipped something from the back of her belt. A headset.

Magnusson looked to Filip. "How about you say goodbye?"

"H—Here? Now?" His glance flitted between Magnusson and the guard.

"That's right." The stoniness of Magnusson's face showed how quickly she would withdraw the offer. She held out her hand. The guard thrust her arm through the hologram, so that Magnusson seemed to hold the headset. Together, they tilted it this way and that, motions synchronized, dangling it like a trainer enticing a dog to perform for a treat.

When Filip reached for it, the hand retracted.

"What happened to Kristine?" Magnusson asked.

Filip swallowed. "Sounds like you already know."

She breathed in deeply—*Why?*—and said, "But I want you to tell it to me."

He thought of the pink blush that graced Kristine's face throughout the long winters. The cackle of her laugh. The feel of her soft hair pressed against his bare chest at night. How she spread out on their hard tweed couch, wrapped in that blanket she knitted to keep her hands

84

busy. There she remained for months, chewing on rice cakes, popping her prescribed pills on days when she remembered. The weak smile she'd give him when he sat beside her, pinched her nose.

He lowered his head, the weird shame of grief taking over his face. "We met when I lived in Trondheim." He clasped his hands. "She was a law student. Supposedly. She didn't last long."

Magnusson's hand retreated as if tired. The guard's hand followed.

"Depression," he said.

"Terrible disease."

He made a fist with one hand and gripped it with the other. "I took time off work to look after her. All she could do was play videogames—so that's all we did together."

He looked to Magnusson, whose expression remained the same—meanwhile, he was close to breaking.

"I loved her so much," he added.

Magnusson exhaled with something like satisfaction, and the guard held out the headset.

He accepted it, put it on and adjusted the tightening knobs.

Marina's room had white walls this time. Acoustic tiles lined the ceiling. She wore a white jumpsuit, like a prisoner or test subject. An expression of remorse drooped her face.

He looked only at the square aluminum table between them, at her warped reflection in it as she spoke.

"I'm sorry, Filip."

He froze, short-circuiting as he tried to make sense of what she meant. Was he talking to himself? A memory of Kristine? Some unknowable combination thereof?

"You would've learned eventually." She reached out a hand, which hovered over his. "You have all the strength you need to move on. Forgive me for keeping that a secret."

"What?"

"That you never needed me at all."

He pulled at the elastic strap to leave space for tears falling off his face.

"You really won't look at me?" she asked.

He took off the headset, intent on protecting his further grief from Magnusson's apparent absorption.

As he headed back towards the door in embarrassment, he dried his face on his sleeve.

The guard stuck out an arm and spoke for the first time: "I'll escort you out."

—

Back in his apartment, head in a fog, Filip went to his racing chair and pulled the blocky console out of the back of it.

"Hello, Filip," the AI assistant said.

The screen turned on and a yellow bouncing ball of an avatar sent ripples across a green synthetic sea.

He headed to his balcony. It had gone without use all winter, the wicker chairs carelessly weathered by months of wind and snow. He looked down at the clear bubbles of protected greenery beneath his balcony, cranking his arm back, ready to throw the last of Kristine crashing through the glass below.

He stopped and placed the console on a nearby chair heap. "Hang on."

Back inside, he took his phone out and swiped it to sync with his home system. The image he snapped from Psychome HQ expanded on the TV screen.

The AI scanned it and returned a list of potential interpretations: coordinates, serial numbers, prime numbers, strings of code, ciphers—

One was a Georgian phone number.

"Can you call that, please?"

A green phone icon pulsed on the screen, soon replaced by the image of a middle-aged woman on a blurry connection. Behind her was beige patterned wallpaper and three ugly framed plates with roses round their rim. She pulled a shawl over her arms, put her reading glasses on and stared at the camera.

Filip held his arms up in apology. "Sorry."

She shook a finger and said something.

AI translated her speech, which scrolled along the

bottom of the screen. "No marketing!"

She searched for the end call button.

"Wait! Does the name 'Marina' mean anything to you?"

She gasped and said something else. Ellipses appeared at the screen's corner as the AI translated.

He got up and pulled out the steel drawer beneath the TV, searching through the mess of cables and outdated gaming paraphernalia within: old controllers, tattered handbooks, dead batteries. Somewhere at the bottom was his translator bud. He put it in his ear and clipped the attached mic to his shirt. It was faster this way.

"You know where my daughter is?" the woman asked. "You have to tell me!"

"No. But I—I'm looking for her."

The woman looked him up and down. "The police will find her first, so keep out of it. I'm recording our conversation and I'll send it to them afterwards. They'll know what to do with you, whoever you are."

"I don't know what you're thinking, but I'm on your side."

"I've heard that before."

"But I—I really do know her. She, she told me about your dumplings."

The woman frowned. Had it translated properly?

"Her favorite food," he continued. "She dipped them in mayonnaise and vinegar. No chance I'd forget that. Or even think of it myself."

Marina's mother lowered her head.

Filip waited for her to compose herself.

"I've got your number," she said eventually. "I've seen your face. If you make this worse—though I don't see how you can—I'll send the police after you the same, okay?"

"I—" He gripped his head in his hands, then dropped his arms to his side again. "Fine. Please, just tell me what you know."

She sat up straight. "Okay. I think it started with this Norwegian woman she met at a party. At least she said she was Norwegian. Marina showed me a photo once. Pretty, blonde, blue eyes. Though I guess they all are." She added, as if to herself, "Never left this country." Then back to Filip: "This friend of Marina's, she said she was an exchange student. Marina must have told her she was struggling to get a job, because the woman said Marina should go with her when she returned to Norway. That they could get an apartment together and it would be easy to get a better paying job than here." She swallowed. "I told her it seemed suspicious. But she'd been unemployed for almost two years. And promised to send money once she found a job. Times are tight here, as I'm sure you've heard."

He didn't know what she meant but nodded to keep her talking.

She adjusted her glasses. "I haven't heard from Marina since. I keep phoning the police in Oslo, but they don't know anything." She stood up and left, returning with a notepad, which she held up to the screen. It was an address in town.

Filip got up and double tapped the TV's corner, so it took a screenshot.

"Where is that?" He asked.

"It's where—" She shook her head. "Please. Before I go on, you have to tell me when you last saw her. Is she okay?"

Filip shuddered, thinking what to say, his ears ringing with dread. He regained control of his breath.

As the ringing diminished, he heard the rain battering down.

He dashed towards the balcony and slid back the glass door. "One second!"

He picked up the console and pressed it to his shirt to dry it off, hoping that nothing had yet corroded.

The TV buzzed. The call had dropped.

"Thank God."

He placed the console on his racing chair and prepared to leave again.

—

The address Marina's mother provided led Filip beyond the old solar shipyard at the tip of Aker Brygge. He tripped on the occasional discarded solar cell, nestled within the overgrown thicket of weeds poking through the stone walkway. Moonlight reflected a wobbling strip of light along the water and glinted on an angular golden statue at the harbor, which looked like the nerves of a giant tooth. Darkness crowded all around, save for cones of light between dim spotlights in disrepair. Did anyone come here anymore? The sound of footsteps echoed between the buildings—or was it crumbling bricks, scurrying animals?

Filip jerked with fear as his phone rang. Nils again. At best, he was looking to apologize. At worst, he planned to bring Filip in for further testing.

Filip put his phone back in his pocket, unanswered. He tugged his jacket close to his chest as he walked towards the formerly sleek apartment blocks of the residential area, their exposed metal girders now wind-bitten and rusty, windows pocked with water spots. His eyes flitted to glance at anything that moved: leaves in the breeze, hanging wires, a fox.

At the address was a Chinese restaurant. It seemed abandoned at first, the wood of its façade rotting, Styrofoam takeaway packaging crunched into dirty piles on its patio. But its charcoal-coloured steel door was new. As Filip got closer to it, the same strange interlocking hexagons of Marina's tattoos shimmered darkly.

Beneath the door handle was a keypad. He took Nil's building pass out and held it there.

Click.

Had the door unlocked so easily?

Metal pressed against the back of his head. The sound was a gun's safety coming off.

"Filip." A woman's voice.

An arm reached out in front of him, pressing a newer card to the reader. The face of the guard from Psychome HQ. The reader beeped and the door swung open. The guard pushed him in.

Inside, there was a single leather chair in the center of a concrete floor. The walls had shelves set into them, their metal handles glimmering. Moonlight spilled in from cracks in the walls.

The gun pushed him forward a few steps and the lights turned on. To his right, there was a wall of screaming faces on TV screens. Beside each was as small graph, a line upon it moving down, down. The faces jump-cut, like badly looped footage. They seemed calmer each time they appeared. It looked to Filip like a video game test, a simulation training the faces to be more docile.

A long tank ran beneath the screens, filled with some opaque green fluid. Eddies of mist rose from circular openings, through which a mess of cables and tubing streamed out in disarray.

Immersed in the fluid were brains, each in a customized plastic case that mapped the grooves of their surfaces. Each case was in a battery farm-liked wire cage. Some fluid from a distributing manifold ran between the plastic casing and the brains.

He tried to look without turning his head.

"Ready to join them?" The guard said.

Adrenaline stole Filip from his body. He spun around and grabbed at the gun.

Bang.

A flash lit up the gaunt mask of the guard's face, the same one from Psychome's HQ. He fell to the floor, scurrying back on his heels, shaky hands searching his chest and arms.

The shot had missed.

She ushered him towards the chair with the gun's smoking tip. He crawled backwards, shuffling his way up the chair's warm wet leather, the smell of ammonia burning in his nostrils.

She walked to a set of shelves in the wall, removing a roll of duct tape. Without a word, she wrapped strips of it around his arms and legs, binding him to the chair.

Squeak.

He cringed. It was a piece of machinery that the guard wheeled towards him. When it emerged from the darkness, he screamed.

A metal halo, replete with needle-like projections, lowered towards his head. The needles, attached to long plastic tubing filled with that same sickly fluid from the tank, craned backwards as they prepared for insertion.

"Hey!"

That voice—it was Nils.

In a flash, Nils ran beyond Filip, towards the woman at the back, out of sight again. Filip heard only the machinery whirring above him. The halo expanded and slipped over his forehead, constricting coldly until his veins distended.

Punching. Yelling.

The blade felt like a cool fingernail tracing around the back of his head in one sweep. Warm blood dripped down his skin. The excision began.

He shut his eyes as sparks flew above him and the halo's arm-like extension tugged him around.

The whirring stopped. The needles retracted.

When Filip opened his eyes again, he saw Nils battering the machine with a wrench. It whined and sparked. Strings of its wires sprayed out from its smashed-open structure.

Nils looked back at Filip, panting with relief. "You good?" He unwrapped the duct tape from Filip's limbs.

Filip felt the back of his head and touched blood. He wiped it on his jeans, then hugged his friend.

"You're good," Nils said.

—

A dozen or so police drones buzzed across the water. Two golf ball-sized devices with blue lights had just taken

Nil's and Filip's statements. Tethers dangled from three of the bigger drones, connected to a secure bag with Magnusson's guard in it, her ponytail waving in the breeze as they carted her back to the station. Their spotlights illuminated strips of the harbor's battered buildings, whose dirty, smashed windows resembled moth-eaten curtains.

Filip gripped onto a metal railing, dangling his legs over the water. He wiped his forehead with his hand, clearing the last flakes of blood.

Nils sat beside him, having explored the strange building further. He looked up at the drones.

"Weird that they don't care enough to send humans," Filip said.

Nils tried to slap Filip on the back of the head, but Filip ducked, touching his scalp where the blade had sliced it.

"Sorry!" Nils said. "But, hey. I cared enough to send myself, is my point."

"Did you find out what's going on?"

"Oh yeah." Nils hugged his knees close to his chest. "As per Psychome's many revenue projections, these ghosts—they're so valuable that if you kidnapped someone, they'd be worth more to you dead. And see, there are these vague ads all over the internet offering money-making opportunities abroad. Free travel to get there."

"No."

Nils nodded.

Filip's knuckles blanched as he gripped the railing tighter. "Couldn't you just build a 3D model of some invented person? Give them an AI personality instead?"

Nils coughed. "As someone who's paid for that kinda service, I can tell you, it doesn't compare. At the bar, ghost chips came to me in parcels and I locked them away. I had no reason to suspect, and what was I gonna do anyway? Psychome had me thinking they'd only kept me because they'd hit their firing quota for that quarter or something. So, Magnusson—accompanied by that lackey we just sent to jail—comes to the bar. The lackey gives me Marina's file back. I didn't know they had it. But again, I kept quiet." He tutted at himself. "Well, Magnusson asks me to destroy the file, along with a huge list of ghosts that the lackey hands me. I ask if I can warn the respective customer bases of each ghost first. Magnusson says no. I say I understand. She leaves." He elbowed Filip. "In a stroke of genius, I save Marina on this!" He took a headset from his backpack. "She's jailbroken. Works anywhere! Serves Psychome right for thinking I couldn't code, haha!"

Filip remained reticent, staring with more focus at the bobbing water.

"When you didn't answer your phone, I went to your place." Nils pointed over his shoulder with a thumb.

"That's when I saw this address on the screen."

Filip turned to him. "You got in? To my place?"

"Fil, I've spent as much time chatting to you as I have playing games. You think I don't know how to answer your security questions?"

Filip kicked his legs in thought. "Yeah." He looked to the sky, considering his next words carefully. "I went to the HQ. With your card. And Magnusson told me— told me Marina wasn't real."

"Do I have to spell that one out?"

"She said I'd invented her."

"No way! That's low, that is."

"What?"

"Remember that customer I fought with that time? I got him to leave peacefully, but it took me a while to work out why. I think he figured I'd made a mistake when I said I'd once dated his chosen ghost. Because whoever he described didn't match the woman I knew." Nils punched Filip lightly on the arm. "That's what the headsets do! They use real ghosts but have their behavior and appearance designed by the user's mind. To some extent. They 'meet you in the middle.' I'm pretty sure that's what was going on with those faces on the screens back there."

"Wow."

"What? What are you thinking?"

Filip tutted. "That I shouldn't have involved myself. Marina's just another woman I couldn't save."

"What are you talking about? We shut this down! Who knows how many potential future victims we freed?"

Filip swung his legs up and lay on his belly, looking over the water.

"You okay, dude? Wanna talk to Marina maybe?"

In lieu of a response, Filip retched into the harbor.

—

PSYCHOME FOUNDER CHARGED WITH 'TRAFFICKING SOULS'

The hologram of the disgraced, deceased CEO of Psychome, Dr. Åste Magnusson, was sentenced to deletion in court yesterday, following a bizarre and disturbing list of crimes...

—

Filip winced as he tried to don his mic without touching the bandage around his forehead. Nils helped him adjust it. Together they stood in Filip's living room, in front of the big TV.

Marina's mother appeared on the screen.

"Can you hear us?" Filip said.

She nodded and held up a VR headset.

Nils pointed. "I see you got our package. You ready?"

She placed it on, and the men explained how to adjust it.

She wailed, a stream of Georgian escaping from her.

The black plastic of the headset shielded her eyes, but her mouth opened in awe. "My daughter. That's my daughter."

"Sorry it took us so long to get it to you," Nils said. "We didn't want the mail to get intercepted while the police were still questioning you. Plus, we weren't sure if it was appropriate."

She removed the headset again. "Thank you."

They talked a little longer, vowing to keep in touch, not yet sure why, or how.

"Phew," Nils said as they hung up. "That felt, uh—"

"About as good as any of this is gonna feel." Filip went to the fridge and retrieved a beer for each of them.

Nils accepted one. "There was one more thing I wanted to ask you."

"Yeah?"

"I'm still taking everything in—but something you mentioned stuck with me. That night, by the harbor. You said Marina was 'just another woman you couldn't save.'"

"Ah."

Filip spun the beer in his hands as he told the story of Kristine. As he spoke, they both flopped into beanbags in the room's corner. When he looked up to see if Nils was still paying attention, his friend met him with a soft and reassuring smile.

Filip lowered his head and shook it. "I resented her

for holding me back."

Nils' mouth opened as if to correct this.

"I did. I think she could tell. I woke up one day and she'd overdosed on her anti-anxiety meds."

"Man, I'm sorry."

Filip looked to his bottle, peeling the label in silence.

"It's like me and Laila." Nils looked dreamily at the constellations spinning on the TV screen. He was about to swig his beer, but stopped. "You do remember who Laila is."

"A ghost?"

"Yeah. Police took her, man. Now I don't expect to see her, ever again." Tears welled on his lower eyelids. "I had so many plans."

On the TV now was a screensaver of Supertrak, golden karts speeding along a diamond ribbon.

Nils put his bottle on the floor. "Wait." He examined the leaderboard in the corner and saw Keeks' top time. "Is that the best? I could smash that, easy."

Filip got a restless feeling in his hands. He reached over, grabbing the steering wheel from the floor and tossing it like a discus over to Nils, who caught it.

The pedals and wheels of the racing kit emerged.

And Filip told Nils, "Go ahead."

THE MOTH & FLAME

"Crime," Luis said, "but with a sci-fi twist!" He held up a palm as if to halt the discussion any further until he got out this next essential point: "You know, as I told you about it, I just realised. Maybe the protagonist could be Argentinian! I know of someone who could play him." He winked once more.

Guess it's not all great being Dad, Ben thought. Although I'm happy people are constantly holding him accountable for having to do some sort of work.

As for his attraction to Luis, the cringe did make it slip momentarily. But it came back full force when Ben realised, *Luis is hot* and *fucking stupid! That combo will be the death of me, I swear.*

Luis looked between the unimpressed father and son. "Did—Did I fuck up?" he said. "Should I have brought you guys NDAs first or something?"

Oliver Baring let his mouth hang open, trout-like, eyeing up Luis. He took off his eyeglasses and leaned in towards him. "What you should have done," he said, "is brought us our goddamn desserts in peace, else I would not have had you fired."

"You mean you—oh."

With that, Oliver used the earpiece of his eyeglasses

to point to his empty champagne flute. Luis obliged, filling it again.

"For you, sir." He turned to Dad with a fat red bottle.

"When was the last time you spoke with your mother?" Dad asked Ben.

Okay, I fucked it. That's the end of 'rumor chat.'

Mum, a high school teacher in Glasgow with a creeping alcohol habit—likely to stem the invisible dread of her falling-apart marriage—was just another source of contention between father and son. Another potential avenue of argument.

"Chambord Liqueur Royale de France," Luis continued. "From the Loire Valley—"

"I messaged Mum the last time you read a script," Ben replied.

Dad let out a sharp, ugly laugh in shock.

"You'll, uh, appreciate its velvety texture." Luis poured a little of the blood-red liqueur into its glass, a crystal thimble on a comically long stem. "The complex flavor profile—"

"Mum gets sad when she doesn't hear from you."

"—comes from its blend of dark berry fruits and the infusion of herbs and spices—"

"I get sad if I hear from her."

Dad slammed his hand down.

Gasps from across the adjacent tables. Heads turning. A yelp.

Luis, frozen, was not at all versed in what to do, in whatever scenario this was.

Oliver raised his arms to the heavens as if to invoke God's patience as he launched into one of his prepared monologues: "The opportunities I gave those women! Their children!" He fired a sharp finger in Ben's direction. "So many submissions we receive! I never need toilet paper, I just—"

"'Wipe my arse with CVs.' I remember your line, Dad, but surely they're all emailed PDFs these days."

Luis, without further sommelier filigree, quickly unscrewed the bell-shaped bottle of port and poured it in Ben's glass, ready for a quick getaway.

"Thousands would *love* to be my kid," Oliver concluded, glaring at Ben.

"Is that what you told all those child stars before you felt them up?"

Oliver threw his liqueur in Ben's face.

Palpable silence in the merciful darkness.

Ben licked the syrupy red off his chin. Nicely sweet. Very alcoholic.

He leapt across the table, spilling his port, knocking over the candles, belly flat upon his salsa-coated swordfish plate. Dad's chair tipped backwards with the weight of them both, table falling to the side. Cutlery clanging, crystal smashing.

Ben pinned Dad to the floor, snatched up a steak

knife and stabbed Oliver Baring—of all people!—in the belly.

Father and son looked to one another in shock. All around, eyeballs shimmered darkly in the candlelight, a bobbing sea of onlookers.

Ben had popped the proverbial cork. No forcing it back in the bottle now.

He crawled off his dad and stood up, wiping salsa and port off his lapels, taking in this weird new world in which he now lived.

Dad gasped, clutching the hilt of the blade stuck in his belly. He made to stand up.

"Dad." Ben held a hand out as if advising Dad not to exert himself further.

Dad slowly rose to his feet, his greasy hair falling forwards in wet tendrils. He clutched at his gut. In a slick and sickly sound, he pulled the steak knife back out and brandished its bloody blade at his son. Red bloomed from the wound, soaking into his shirt.

The pair circled one another, knives in hand.

"Oy!" one of the chefs called out from the kitchen. The others quickly discouraged him from heroics.

Oliver, gut drooping over his trousers, squatted like a crab, tossing the knife between hands.

"Dad," Ben said. "It's not too late to—"

Dad darted forwards and slashed his son across the face.

Ben touched at his cheek. Dad had sliced it into two profusely bleeding flaps.

A rictus upon Dad's mouth. Eyes narrowing.

"Call it even." Ben held his face together. "We don't have to—"

Dad lashed out again, landing a slice on Ben's forehead this time. Ben grabbed the offending wrist and punched his knife into Dad's belly once again, deeper than before.

Dad doubled over, coughing. He fell on his side, back on the carpet.

Ben straddled him with the steak knife. "Please."

Why pretend Dad made him do this? He wanted to keep going. To carve the father out of himself.

He pressed his hand against Dad's shirt, positioning the knife between two ribs, over the heart. He held it there, palm on the hilt, ready unless Dad gave him good reason to abstain.

Dad coughed. "You started it."

Ben let out an involuntary laugh. He figured out what was so funny when the words came to him: "You started *me!*"

His palm became a fist that battered down upon the blade, driving it into Dad's heart.

—

"What do we do?"

"Don't meet his eyes!"

"Stay calm."

"Keep quiet."

"No sudden movements."

Ben barked out another sharp laugh.

I'm a patricide, not a bear.

Some patrons froze. Some dashed for the emergency exits or the entrance, whichever was closer. Some sat back down at their tables, lowering their heads.

Ben ignored them all as he staggered back to his table, sitting once again across from his father's conspicuously empty chair.

Luis stood frozen nearby.

Ben looked at the deep slashes across his face in the distorted reflection of a dessert spoon. "Oliver Baring." He looked to Luis. "Middle name 'Fucking.' Has—*had*—to put his mark on everything." He lazily poked at his knocked-over glass of port. "What was this one?"

"O-Oh. Um." Luis picked up the bottle, where Ben had knocked it over when lunging at his dad, and poured Ben a new glass. "Graham's forty-year-old tawny port. Aged in an oak cask. Balance of sweetness and acidity." The shock had locked him back in sommelier mode.

Ben took a sip, savoring it. "Ah. Notes of chocolate. Nuts."

"Yeah." Luis scratched at his neck, looking around. "And caramel and—toffee, can I go now?"

Ben gestured towards the table. "How about dessert?"

"Right." Luis cleared the dinner plates and headed off to the kitchen. He took two desserts from where they lay on the open zinc counter. The chefs all stood open-mouthed, watching. Several were on their phones, presumably to the police. Some were filming—for that LiveLeak cred, no doubt.

Luis returned with two plates, placing one before Ben. "Chocolate truffle terrine."

Ben took his dessert fork and pushed it into the dark, square jelly. It yielded nicely. Inside were beads and pearls of solid chocolate.

He took a bite.

"Fuck that's good."

Not too chewy. Right on the cusp of "too sweet."

Peak mouthfeel. Probably. Whatever that is.

"Dad made the perfect choice. As a kid I loved everything chocolate."

Savoring the terrine, Ben felt like a kid who got good grades on a summer Friday. And he looked, for the first time, on the brink of tears.

"He used to call me—'chocolate jaws.'"

"I just wanted to say."

Ben turned with shock towards Jasmine Blackwood, the sleek and sultry star actor herself, with her long, black, glossy ponytail and shimmering dress. He'd only seen magnified versions of her on IMAX screens before. Still she made a larger impression in person.

"You did the right thing." She ventured a hand forwards, resting it on Ben's shoulder.

Affectionate physical touch! Painfully rare. Always welcome. Even from the most unusual sources, like Jasmine Blackwood. In the most unusual circumstances, like these.

Ben tilted his head, pressing it against her hand to maximize the connection.

"You'll have your supporters," she added. "No matter what happens next."

She slipped her hand out the crook of Ben's neck. Away she went, as quickly as she'd arrived.

Ben leaned down and felt beneath the table. Luis took a step back in surprise, not sure what he was up to.

Ben came back up with Dad's briefcase in hand, gesturing with it to Luis to show what he'd been after.

Inside was Ben's script. Thick, heavy. He flicked through it, spying handwritten notes on every page.

Yes.

✓✓✓

♡♡♡

"What's that?" Luis asked.

"My script."

"What's it about?"

Ben dropped it on the table, startling Luis. "I guess I don't have much time to get into the details, but the gist of it is…"

FOR SALE: TWINK ASS. NEVER WORN; OR, LAS AVENTURAS DE POLLITO Y EL MARICÓN.

"I'm only telling you because we share everything." Tony placed his little bird-boned hand on mine.

We looked over the Sierra Nevada mountains, glassy waters reflecting the cloud-filled skies above, grass down below dotted with firs and pines.

"This could be the start of a career." Tony flicked up his cream-coloured plastic sunglasses, meeting my eyes to add sincerity. "Remember I said that?"

"I do."

He squatted, arms folded over his knees, butt floating over the rock beneath him. His white flannel hoodie and sweatpants were for ladies and two sizes too small. They showed off his ridiculously flat belly, his delicate ankles. White sneakers of course. I'd told him on the trail it would all get dirty, but he was so precious, made us take our time just to keep himself clean.

I pulled my hand from his and grabbed at a nearby twig, tearing it apart. "I thought you were joking. Start of a career," I muttered, unable to meet his eyes. "Pretty fast end to it."

I was in one of my standard black denim, heavy

metal t-shirts. Jeans dirtied, but you're not supposed to wash them. I didn't really wash much of anything, not even myself. Deodorant's not good for you, and those who learn to live without it and stop stripping their skin of its oils, they smell better.

"You can sell it multiple times, though!" Tony said. "It's not a real thing, so how are they supposed to know?" Tony, he takes like multiple full-on baths per day. He's got this set of bags duct-taped in the base of his shower for this express purpose. "Not great for the environment," I'd told him. "What are you talking about?" he had replied. "It's amazing for the environment of people around me. You should try it sometime."

I pressed my hands over my ears, hair held flat against them. "One virginity loss at a time." My thick black hair had started to curl, slowly becoming dreadlocks.

I relaxed my hands, folded them in my lap. "I know you too well to think I can talk you out of this."

"Couldn't even if *I* wanted to. The site's up. Asian twink virginity for sale. Folks are bidding."

"What kind of folks?"

Tony reapplied his lip balm. "Pervy old guys, probably. What would you expect?" He brushed hair out of my face. "Say something, please."

I didn't want to look at him. I knew I'd meet his eyes and there would be my best friend and I'd want to tell him

'Yes' to anything he wanted.

But I didn't want to want that. So, I forced my eyes shut and asked, "Why are you doing this to me?"

"To *you*?"

"Since you met me, your life has never been all about you."

I heard it out loud. It was weird.

Tony stood again, his ropy little muscles likely tired from hunkering down. "I'm just telling you because—I don't know, it's kinda funny, isn't it?"

"It's sad." I stood beside him. "And fucking dangerous." I wrapped one arm over his chest, the other across his forehead. "I mean, if you wanted to lose your virginity so badly…"

I let the thought trail off. I didn't know the answer. I just knew it was—not what he'd planned.

He tried to wrench away of me, but I gripped him harder, growling. He laughed at first, trying to struggle free. But as I tightened my hold he tutted, pissed off for real, and I had to let him go.

A breeze passed by. Bracing, pine scented.

"I don't want to lose my virginity," he said.

"Then—"

"Or—I—it's a made-up thing anyway. A concept I don't believe in." He folded his arms. "Its's about someone who does believe in it paying a lot of money *for* it. And me using that money to pay for college and getting the fuck out of here."

He took my hand in his. He did this a lot. Just a very tactile guy.

The first time, years ago, he'd placed a hand on my thigh without thinking. Afraid, he'd pulled it away, like he'd just plunged his hand into a rock cave and touched a scorpion. I'd smiled, placing his hand back on me. It was just bromance affection or whatever. Unlike like the roughhousing thing I do with him, his touch is—intimate.

But I wouldn't do that back, you know?

I couldn't claim this was the first time we'd discussed something like this. He'd floated it that time we were hiding in the bushes by the Oakwood Golf Course, rich dicks far away like little plastic figures in their pastel tops and white trousers. I realised when I saw them why Tony liked wearing white so much. It was the colour of someone who did no work, expected no physical act to taint his clothes.

White, to Tony, was aspirational.

"One of these esteemed gentlemen," Tony had said then, "would pay to fuck me. Easy." He'd looked to me with full sincerity. "That's the goal. Become a sugar baby while I can."

I'd stifled a snort, trying not to give us away. We weren't supposed to be on the course. I'd clipped my way through a mesh fence to get us here. We had nothing else to do and were amused merely by the feeling of doing something we weren't supposed to.

Tony slapped the back of my neck weakly. "You don't think I could?"

What did I think? Tony was clever, funny, charming. Had a sorta feminine beauty: high cheekbones, flawless skin, brown eyes, platinum blonde hair that the girls at school would quiz me about. "Ryan, his hair is so shiny and straight. Please tell me he straightens it. What products does he use?"

"That's pure Tony, ladies," I'd reply.

They'd sigh with envy and float off again, no interest in me whatsoever.

At the golf course I'd said to him, "Tony, I think you could do anything you wanted. But that's the thing. *Would* you want to do that?"

He'd had no time to complete that thought. One of the golfers had spotted us and we'd had to dip.

That had been the end of that.

Until now.

"Please," Tony said finally, "just tell me what you're thinking. Whatever it is."

I was thinking that he and I came from a great legacy of wasters, all of us born against our will, thrust from the wombs of monsters across the wasteland of Sacramento, scrabbling for mere survival and rarely anything more. Doing only what we knew, what our forefathers did. And what was that? Nothing good, that's for sure.

"I think I want to go home," I replied.

Tony tried to hold my gaze assertively. But his mouth did that little screwed up thing when he was super concerned but didn't know what to say.

He flicked his sunglasses back down. "Well, okay then."

And we headed back up the trail towards my car.

—

Sacramento. Noun: "Religious ceremony imparting divine grace."

Greta Gerwig made that movie about hating it.

The *My Favourite Murder* women describe it as some sort of culture-void crimehub.

Joan Didion was from here and loathed it too.

I think. Honestly I can barely understand that woman. Tony loaned me *The White Album* and said it would change my life. It sure did: I never knew such simple sentences, composed of words I understood, could be so fucking dull and incomprehensible.

After that we'd had a frank discussion about how he could get porn on his phone anytime he wanted. I was genuinely concerned he had forgotten, what with this fucking book he'd lent me.

Well look, I don't know the long-ago history of the place. I just associate it with my own shitty upbringing, the occasional serial killer—makes perfect sense that residents get so bored they start chopping each other up and drinking blood just for something to do—and fuck all else.

—

I don't have many memories of Eastbrook Heights Mobile Home Park—yes, that one—before Tony arrived. But I have to imagine it was as chaotic then as now. Creepers peeping in windows. Drunken arguments and parties. Weirdos blasting music out their phones, shotgunning beers, smashing bottles against the side of our trailer sometimes.

With such a legendarily bad reputation you might wonder why, if our home was so damn mobile, Mom didn't cart us off somewhere else?

She used to work as a foreman—foreperson?—at one of the few flatpack furniture manufacturing places in the US. Until a forklift flatpacked her foot. After that, disability checks for life. They offered her some course on how to find meaning once you didn't have to work anymore, but she was already in the bar celebrating. A decade and a half later—Mom always in a ratty housecoat, 'nips' of this and that filling her pockets—the celebration continued.

Tony moved in when I was five.

He was the son of Chinese immigrants. Very sweet couple. Couldn't speak English at the time. We had to communicate through good vibes alone, but there were plenty of those.

Tony was the youngest of four brothers, the elder three a good decade older than him at least. So he felt kinda left out. As an only child, so did I.

We'd play Bakugan in the wet mud between our trailers. We'd run off to a nearby pond and lob stuff in. We'd see who could splash the highest, make the most satisfying *gloop* sound as our rock hit the water. Sometimes it was old burst tires that we rolled wonkily off a cliff. We'd climb up trees and I'd trap him between the branches, tickling him until he puked.

When it rained, we'd watch The Price is Right, Wheel of Fortune, Jeopardy! They lit the people on TV so brightly, so colourfully, like they were from another dimension.

Later we traded Bakugan for D&D. I was dungeon master for Tony and a few other local kids. We had to stop when I learned that none of them liked it, they were just afraid of me.

I'd steal cash from Mom and we'd grab an Uber, head to the city centre. We once ended up outside some arena where Taylor Swift was playing—Tony's idea. When we couldn't sneak in, we joined a party in the adjacent parking lot, everyone but me singing along to her music. I got my first kiss that night: Savannah, a girl from San Francisco. She wore a long, tie-dyed t-shirt, scrunchie in her hair, short denim skirt, and dirty white sneakers. She tasted like bubblegum.

One time, when Tony's parents were at work, we hung out with his older brothers. It was about the only time I ever spoke to them and they all moved out soon enough—but not before they showed us what sites we could look up on our phone. That day, Tony and I learned how to jerk off.

I'm realising now that maybe Tony could only 'get there' because *I* was there. I won't ask him though. I'm not ready for the answer. I think it would hurt either way.

—

Tony had this depressed period. I felt bad for him at first but, God, I have to admit it was fucking annoying, too. You couldn't say that to him, it just set him off again. Nothing made him feel better but plenty made him worse.

He retreated into himself, wouldn't see me anymore. I let him do that for a while to see if that would work but it didn't. So, I banged on his trailer door, insisting he come see me.

He said we should go for a walk, so I took us to Crestwood Hills, a nearby forest area we'd never bothered to visit before.

Once we were in the thicket, nothing but dim moonlight shooting through the firs surrounding us, he said, "I'm gay."

I was furious. I knew he could read it on my face, instantly, that there was no hiding that from him.

He dashed away from me, back towards the park.

I tackled him, held onto his legs. He tried to struggle free, calling, "No! Help! Help!"

I had to crawl atop him and secure one hand across his mouth just to shut him up. "Tony, would you calm the fuck down?" I had to speak quickly. "*That's* the reason you've been so depressed, didn't want to see me?"

He nodded, tears leaking out his eyes.

"Tony," I said, "one, I already knew. I have eyes."

Fastest-walking kid in Sacramento, decked out in pearls and fake Versace?

"Two—that's fucking stupid."

He took this in. He sat up, hugging his knees to his chest, catching his breath, stifling his sobs, wiping his eyes.

We sat there on the soft floor of wet earth and decaying bark. "You gotta promise me one thing."

"This doesn't change anything?"

"It already has. It's been weeks and you've refused to hang out with me. But it won't change anything again. Okay?"

I held out a hand for him to shake on our agreement. He held his out. I pulled him to his feet and we both walked back to the park.

"Fucking drama queen," I muttered, and he laughed.

Only Mom had something to say about it. What people would think and all that.

"Fuck people, man!" I'd replied. "People *don't*

think."

—

Once we were old enough—fourteen—we joined Noah and Mason, the perma-partying dudes a few trailers down from ours. We'd chip in money for beers and they'd hand us some. We'd drink and dance and they'd tell us stories about their biker gang days, how they got in tussles with the cops. The shady character who had tried to hire them to beat up his ex-wife 'to teach her a lesson.' They'd show us scars on their chests and torsos, claiming they were bullet wounds. It was probably all bullshit from two over-the-hill, lesion-coated losers, but they told such great stories that we didn't care.

By then Tony was comfy enough being himself with most. He was effete, flirtatious, and engaged in a kind of overtly sexual humour that he would scale back in future years. He was just excited to be accepted not only for who he was, but for a little *more* than he was. He was pushing that boundary in his own way. So was I with my excessive cursing, drinking until I puked, my angsty nihilistic rants. It was the cringiest of times for us both.

Noah and Mason didn't give a shit. The closest they came to bringing up Tony's sexuality was when Mason, watching Tony lip sync to Dolly Parton, said, "He's one of them boy-girls."

We all laughed. Because, yeah! That was Tony. He was one of them boy-girls.

Noah and Mason always partied later than us. We'd leave them to it, climb up on top of my trailer—no waking Mom, no chance—and have those pseudo-philosophical debates we loved when we were still drunk and sometimes stoned.

"This notion," I'd begin, "that it's brave, actually, to live an ordinary life. It's just consolation for a truly meaningless existence, isn't it? Some things are just objectively not worth doing."

Tony, ever the optimist, would reply something like, "I don't think so. There are reports of prisoners of war, victims of hideous crimes, grief-stricken folk left behind by lost loved ones, finding meaning in the most meaningless of places."

Sacramento certainly qualified.

Tony would hold his hands up, making a frame from his thumbs and index fingers as if capturing all the stars above him. "There is meaning, and there is no meaning. There are no gradients. No meaningful ones at least."

He'd wink at me, and that would be the end of that.

—

Not to say that everyone was as accepting of us as Noah and Mason. As our parents (eventually.) As we were of each other.

I had my long hair, my Mexican appearance. I wore denim cut-off jackets with death metal patches on them. Strangers would yell 'Trump!' at me on the street, if only because they knew 'fag' was unacceptable.

Kids at school though, they used the word liberally. Yeah! They still do that, if you were wondering.

I figured the bullying was less about hating someone else's sexuality than venting frustration about a lack of pussy.

And so Elijah, Jackson and Caleb had to be the most pussy-less motherfuckers in the whole school. Preppy, clean-shaven, square-jawed maniacs, like if you made a horror movie starring Logan Paul as a scientist who clones mutated versions of himself. Almost like white supremacists—except to qualify, they'd need to be educated enough, even in a bad ideology—and genuinely care about *something.* But my bullies were too mindless for shit like beliefs or purpose.

They started with the name-calling like all the rest, but then it escalated. Soon Tony and I were not "fags" but *Pollito y el Maricón.*

"The chicken and the faggot," believe it or not. Tony was *Pollito* because his mom had dressed him as a chicken once for an easter photo session at kindergarten, and also because of slang I'd never heard of: chicken, chickenhawk, chickenhead.

I was *Maricón,* for less creative reasons.

Our nicknames were in Spanish because they slipped the attention of more teachers that way. I also assumed this somehow made them more derogatory.

Tony, positive in outlook as ever, tried to appropriate the slurs used against us. "Ready for the continued adventures of *Pollito y el Maricón*?" he'd say each time I knocked on his trailer, picking him up for our next aimless drive.

This was the start of his platinum blonde hair, blue-contacts phase. He was trying 'to look *super*natural.'

I'd force a smile at his attempted wisecrack, appreciating the attempt more than the execution.

By then I was working at BudgetBarn. I'd saved up a bit and gotten us a run-down Chevrolet Caprice Classic, a written-off police cruiser that I saved from the scrapyard because Tony, of all people, knew a guy who knew a guy. It had rusting wheel arches, cracked leather seats, and took a few cranks of the ignition to start up, but it did the job.

I'd drive us around and Tony, with the aux cord plugged into the dash, would sing along to Madonna, Lana del Rey, and Taylor Swift. I'd play him death metal bands I found on Spotify, like Kama-Mara, Cursed Dominion, and Necrocrush. A fair deal that way: both of us were similarly displeased.

The car's sound system quickly went crackly and quietened down with each play to nothing, so Tony played music out his phone, which slid around on the cracked dashboard. He'd complain that the music would sound amazing out of decent speakers, or at a concert. He was always thinking about life could be better. About the 'good future to come.' Always talking about 'going somewhere.'

Where did he get such ideas?

I *never* assumed I was going anywhere.

I'd never met anyone who had.

On our journey, I'd tell him about the people I met at my job. BudgetBarn was price-competitive even with Walmart. So, imagine: if you paid Target prices to avoid Walmart people, you paid Walmart prices to avoid BudgetBarn people. At its most innocent were the kids taking selfies in the meat aisle because they liked the lighting. There was the middle-aged homeless woman who shouted, "I'm an axe-wound!" over and over and constantly stole, never bothering to conceal the headphones, Nintendo Switch, spatula or whatever it was. I just let her. I think she would have stopped if I'd given her attention, but I didn't feel like it. I figured someone would spot it on the security camera and reprimand me for being in the vicinity and doing nothing, but they never did. If they didn't care, why should I? The worst of my job was scooping up human shit—not even in the toilets or anything, just on the store floor itself. I became something of a feces connoisseur in this time and I can tell you, from the varied consistency and smells, that the shit I dealt with had to have come from multiple different people. Thankfully, unlike Ms. Axe-Wound, I never caught these others committing their crimes.

Tony and I would head off to thrift stores in search of new clothing. Both of us have, to date, spent our lives decked out only in the second-hand. We just grew up doing it and came to love it more than regular shopping, always ending up with the cheapest and most unique stuff. I'd buy new torn black jeans, high top sneakers, worn plaid shirts, and black metal t-shirts—some from bands I knew, others I didn't.

Tony was always on the hunt for the designer and the knockoff designer. Louis Vuitton, Prada, Gucci, Tom Ford. Gaudy, ugly stuff that, I swear, would look terrible on *anyone*. But it did draw the most attention.

Cinnamon, a black trans woman who sold mostly fake handbags out the trunk of her car, always had the best gear. Once, chatting in her garage, she mentioned that her boyfriend was a drug dealer. So, we started going in the house after Tony's spending spree and picking up an eighth of weed each. Mom told me the local stuff was laced with fentanyl. "Cool," I replied. "Maybe it'll kill me."

Sometimes Tony would come into money for gas. He'd just have it, notes of crumpled cash in his loose, pale little fist. We'd convert the cash to fuel and a few forties and head on out to some local quarry, swimming hole or junkyard where the few other high school kids we liked had a barbecue or a 'party' (more forties, one or two

Bluetooth speakers). We'd get drunk and high and take in the panoramic sky. About the only good thing Sacramento had, and it shared it with the rest of the world.

If there were enough crumpled bills in Tony's hand, I'd take him out to San Francisco. We'd wander around, trying to take in the high-rise buildings without rubbernecking like rubes.

Later in the evening, we'd sneak Tony into the gay bars. I needed him to see what life was like elsewhere. Eastbrook was just a stopgap for him; he was destined for greater. He'd stick out from the pack, even in San Francisco.

We'd stumble out—either when the clubs closed or bouncers rumbled us for being underage—and head to the alley where I'd parked the car. I'd let Tony sleep in the back and drape myself across the two front seats, jacket balled over the stick shift. Still it would poke my spine all night. Exhausted from drinking and dancing and the heat, I could always pass out.

Cops often woke us up, knocking on the window in the morning. "You boys better get out of here."

"Oh no," Tony would say, voice rich with camp, "did we do something *bad*, officer?"

Sometimes they'd try and educate us, telling us we were lucky it was them, your friendly neighbourhood police officers, and not someone more malicious.

Hah! Who the fuck could be more malicious than

cops? Suspecting the answer was 'nobody,' I never brought this up.

We'd wash ourselves in the sink of the nearest Starbucks bathroom in the morning then get back in the car, heading home.

On other occasions, just driving around the highways, if Tony was feeling indulgent, he might let me vent about not having a girlfriend. "If only everyone didn't think I was a fag."

Their word, not mine.

"What about Clarissa?"

"That mopey-ass Jesus freak? I'm trying to get laid here, Tony."

"Virginity isn't a real thing, so why stress about losing it?" he'd say. One time he tapped my forearm with his fingers and added, "This might be TMI but—"

"When have you cared about that?"

"Hah. Well look, if you don't care for the person— and I never have—it's like *being* jerked off, instead of *jerking* off. Not so different that you should give as much of a shit as you do."

Sometimes I'd let him leave it at that. One time I added, "But what if no one ever wants to jerk me off?"

He laughed, but I was kinda serious.

"*I* do!" Tony replied.

I scoffed. "You know what I mean."

"But *you* don't know what *I* mean." Tony preened

himself, adjusting his hair. "If *I* want to, some beautiful woman will want to as well. You just need to find her." He smiled. "And you will."

—

This was all a nice antidote to the bullying. But nicknames were soon the least of my problems.

Elijah, Jackson, and Caleb, they started confronting me in the bathroom.

At first it was, "Sure you're in the right place? Didn't you know that soon it'll be illegal for pussies like you to piss in urinals?"

I'd give it, "Yeah yeah," and move on.

But one day Jackson couldn't help but add, "Why not enjoy your last taste?" And smashed my head against the urinal's porcelain, breaking my nose.

He just had that vicious look about him—muscles all constantly tense, bursting at the seams with rage at, who the fuck knows? Everything?

He dunked my head in the commingling piss of so many students. Acrid, ammoniacal—hey, a rare use of English and science class!—combined with the chemical of the urinal cake that dried out my tongue. The iron of blood from my lips where they cut on my teeth.

Memories tying to senses. Traumatic tastes all.

They spotted me after school another day, waiting for Tony to get out of math. Elijah and Caleb took my arms while Jackson had me hold my leg over the edge of the curb. He stamped on it over and over, trying to break it. It didn't make any kind of satisfying sound—and neither would I, determined not to give him what he wanted—just the dull thud of foot connecting with meat. I reckon he fractured it at least.

When Tony showed up, saw me limping and drowsy-looking, he called us an Uber. He tried to get me to the emergency room, but I made him take us straight home.

—

Dr. Perez, an elderly Mexican dude, would come by the trailer each month or so. It was some initiative of his to get uninsured people healthcare.

I lay on my couch and let him examine my leg. He recommended a visit to my GP, who would probably get me an X-ray.

"No shit, Doc," I replied.

It didn't hurt as much by then, but it did still feel raw, like the skin was open. And I was limping as much as I ever had, as I still do. The leg itself was creaky-sounding, no other way of explaining it.

"I can't pay to fix this."

"You know," Dr. Perez said, "if you're getting extensively bullied about your sexuality, it's only natural you start questioning it yourself."

Others around the trailer park must have been yapping about it.

I held out a hand, palm up, as if to say, *The fuck,*

Doc? "I don't need to talk to you about that. But I could use a way of getting out of school for good. For my survival, man. I can't do this."

"Have you told the school about this? Local law enforcement, maybe?"

"Say I told them," I said, tapping my palm with an index finger, "and it didn't work out. What do you think the kids would do to me next?"

He placed a comforting hand on my shoulder. "I can support you through this process."

"Get your fuckin' hands off me, faggot!"

I said that. I didn't know why.

"Sorry," I said eventually. "Just—maybe you can take me on as an apprentice, right? Get me out of school that way? Doesn't it work like that?"

"Apprenticeships are an option. Not necessarily with me, but—maybe this is a discussion you'd better have with your parents?"

My face fell. It was midday on a Sunday and Mom was passed out in the bedroom.

I lowered my head to one side, glaring at the doctor.

"Maybe check out some local businesses that might offer an appropriate apprentice sponsorship for you." He headed for the door. "Before I go, should I examine your nose?"

By this point, it had already set crooked after my encounter with the urinal.

"You could have a deviated septum."

I pressed my hands to my cheeks. "Call Nine-one-one!" I laughed.

On his way out, he shot me a glance of unmistakable pity.

—

Tony said my crooked nose gave my face even more character. "More fool them!" He'd run a fingertip down the bridge of it. "They found a way to make you even more good-looking."

But Tony wasn't always around to make me feel better about myself. And Mom, she was never around.

One night when I couldn't sleep—thoughts not so much racing as looping on one particular, hideous idea—I felt like I couldn't breathe, like something was trapped beneath my skin trying to get out. So I bolted to the kitchen, pulled out a blade and—let it out. The pressure of life. I bled it from my skin.

When Elijah, Jackson and Caleb pulled back my long sleeves they said "Ew, he's one of those mad self-harmers. How do you do it?" Jackson took out his switchblade. "Like this?" He sliced my wrist, deeper than I ever had before, biting the wound and sucking on it.

He wiped my blood off his lips. "What do you think? Do I have pussy powers now? Or just plain-old AIDS?"

Elijah and Caleb laughed.

My right wrist and hand—like my right leg—felt a

bit slower after that. It could be psychological, I'm not sure.

Luckily, I'm a lefty.

Don't think I didn't ask why these three gentlemen were like this—but dwelling on it was a path to madness.

Sometimes folks are wrong in the head. So, you grin and bear them.

I was glad the more severe bullying bypassed Tony. He mattered more to me than I did to myself. Also, maybe I was jumpy and shaky and had hideous nightmares and cut myself and all that—but I was still here. I was in control. I knew I could handle it. I didn't know if Tony could. So even if it had been a choice—bully Tony this badly or bully me—I would've chosen me, every time.

Though I did often wonder: why *didn't* they bully him?

—

And why did the bullying simmer down soon after that vampiric attack?

Was it because I was limping now, scarred on my wrists and face? They figured they'd done enough damage? I wasn't sure. Whatever the reason, I was thankful.

But I also wondered if it was because Jackson's crew were scheming something worse for both of us.

They say if a pet cobra starts lying its length beside you, you have to give him away. He's sizing you up to see if he can eat you. He might not be hurting you directly, but he is scheming about it. And that's when you have to take action.

So, I saved up and bought myself a Beretta M9. Kept it in the glovebox of my car, sealed closed with duct tape. The latch was broken before I bought it.

Just for my protection. It's not like I wanted to shoot up the school or anything.

Well, actually it was exactly like that. But I hoped I wouldn't.

When Tony and I were driving around one time, he tried to put his purse in the glovebox and spied the gun. "I know what you're thinking," he said to me.

I kept my eyes on the road. The rolling hills, the dying light of dusk.

"Don't bless them," Tony said, "by linking their names with yours forever in history. They are far from worthy of that."

I knew he was right and I hoped I didn't end up like them, fighting them the way they fought me. I wanted to double down on being nothing like them.

But so much of life is out of our control.

—

The uncertainty of this period of peace, and my anticipation of its inevitable end, carried on.

In a way it was worse than the bullying. It was an assault of the imagination that I did to myself.

Tony would walk me to school and we'd have to stop so I could vomit down a lane on the way there.

He'd hold my hair aside with his effete little hands. "My handsome boy," he'd say. "Can't be good for your teeth, all this."

One day I told him, "I can't do this anymore."

He remained silent. Must have seen it coming. Knew I had a plan. So, I told him how I would get out of finishing my GED, even though I was failing pretty much everything.

As if that had anything to do with being set up for adult life anyway. They never taught me about taxes, addiction, psychopathy, or anything I'd seen genuinely fuck up the lives of those older than me.

Tony stretched his arms to the sky, his t-shirt pulling up to his navel. "Where to first, then?"

"You can't come with me."

I was, in spite of everything, always proud to be seen with Tony. That didn't mean I wanted to be responsible for subjecting him, to what people would say, at the places I planned on visiting.

I told him something similar. He always knew what I meant. That I was—I don't know, faithful to him like that. In the same way he was faithful to himself.

He placed his hand on mine in that way he liked to do. It felt almost more sensitive because of how little pressure he applied.

"Trust me on this," he said. "We're better together. Besides, it'll get me out of school for the day."

"Don't pretend you don't love it."

"I do," he said. "But I love you more."

—

We toured businesses in the area. Carpenter, electrician, some nearby farms, a solar panel start-up. All of them wanted to give me the 'stay in school' speech.

We even wound up at SnapFit Solutions, where Mom used to work.

"Hey!" I'd heard about Aiden from Mom. He was the new foreman, a thin and wiry-looking man, probably in his late thirties. He walked over to us at the warehouse entrance. Behind him, big industrial machines sawed pine into sheets. "You're Quinn's son."

"Yeah," I said, "That's me." *Fuck yeah!* I thought. *I've landed one!*

"She know you're here?" he asked.

I went in for a joke: "She doesn't know anything anymore."

He let out an involuntary sound like, "Yeugh," and walked away from me.

I too was so saddened by my quip that I had to leave too.

The place just radiated shame.

—

We ended up at Road Medics, a car repair workshop. We

walked confidently past the garage floor towards the office at the back, to meet with the owner, Mr. Reyes.

He was an overweight white-haired guy with callused, cracked hands and deep bags under his eyes like he'd seen some capital S *Shit*. And with him we had the same conversation we'd had so many times that day:

"You're trying to get out of school?"

"Trying to start my life," I said. "Eager to enter the workforce."

He held up a hand. "Listen, son."

People were in two minds about my plan. One was, 'Fuck school, I never used anything I learned there either.' The more common was, 'Don't end up like me, sonny.'

What did that mean about adults in the workforce? That so many saw their own lives as cautionary tales?

From the inflection in Mr. Reyes' voice, the way he leaned on one knee, his sad little 'God give me strength' look to the ceiling, I could tell what flavour of speech I was about to receive.

You couldn't take it seriously. Adults fucking loved to complain. Nice lives, bad lives—they all just fucking hated life, God knew why.

But I turned towards the door. I had no intention of hearing this once more.

I had no intention of becoming an apprentice anywhere. I knew only what I didn't want: to be part of their shitty system where everything sucked but there was no apparent alternative.

Tony, who had slipped in behind me, placed a hand on my shoulder. "I can take it from here."

After that, looking between them, I could no longer 'read the air' in that office. The energy went weird, quick.

Something was about to happen that I didn't want to see.

So I left, heading back across the workshop floor.

"Where's your boyfriend?" said one of the greasemonkeys.

Husky dudes were popular in certain bars Tony and I had gone to in SF, but even this guy was pushing it. I doubted he was popular with any gender. Maybe that was why he was so scornful.

I just smiled at him and nodded as I walked past.

"Alright, easy!" he yelled. "I wasn't coming onto you, cunt. Eyes to the ground!"

At the curb, I sat down, hugging my knees to my chest. Behind me were the sounds of tinny radios, manly shouts, whirring machinery, spraying sparks.

Tony soon shamelessly minced his way back out the garage, to a slew of wolf-whistles.

I checked my phone—flip-type, physical buttons, broken screen—to see that only four minutes had passed.

Tony pulled the permission slip out the back pocket of his tight jeans. "Tada!"

I got up, hugged him and we jumped around in victory. "Do I want to know how?" I asked.

"Standard," Tony said, flipping his sunglasses down coolly. "Asked if his wife blew him anymore. '*Anymore?*' he replied." He shrugged. "So, I—"

"So, you what?"

He just looked at me and cocked his head. "My mysterious gas money? The phone I got you? Our Netflix account?"

"Our *Netflix account?* But we've been using it for years!"

He punched me playfully on the shoulder. "Feel good about that. We definitely got our money's worth."

Tony always had money. Tony always knew a guy who knew a guy. And he'd never said how.

Now I understood why he'd had us visit so many establishments that day. He was tuning into the possibility of sexual bargaining.

For me.

Tony lowered his voice. More serious now. "Did you never wonder why I wasn't bullied?"

"What are you talking about? They say bad stuff about you all the time."

"But none of them ever acted on it with me the way they did with you."

"This is ridiculous."

"*You're* ridiculous, Ryan." He shoved me.

The mechanics gathered to watch, laughing, elbowing each other.

Tony pursed his lips. "I could have spared you the injuries if you'd just told me what Jackson and his cronies were up to. Don't you remember what you told me when I came out? That we would never let things change between us by keeping secrets?"

I looked to the floor. "We both let that happen again."

Tony reached out a hand to my chin, made me look at him. "Don't put this on me. I never explained my plan to give you plausible deniability. So that when it came to this conversation we're having right now you could say"—naturally he put on a dopey voice to imitate me—"'Oh, no, I never would have let you do that.'" He let go of my face, lowering his voice. "I guess I'm done letting you turn a blind eye to this."

I didn't know what to say. Tony was this precious little doll of a person to me.

But okay, we shared many similar experiences. We were far from naive. I knew people either used or got used. I guess I just wanted a different path for us both.

And when I say 'both' I mean 'Tony.' I barely gave a fuck about myself. But Tony, Tony was special. He had an energy about him. A peace. A star quality.

So, I'd always felt it was my responsibility to keep him in his little fantasy world of pop stardom and designer labels. I knew some therapist or school counsellor would hear that and reply, 'But where did you get that idea from?' As if, the idea having come from myself was somehow less legitimate.

Where does *anyone* get their ideas?

Point is, whether Tony agreed—whether it was even *true*—I felt like I'd failed him.

Unable to undo what Tony had done to himself, for us, I started crying profusely. Hands shaking, I sat back down slowly, burying my face in my lap, holding my hands behind my head, breath hitching in my throat.

Tony sat beside me, rubbing my back, comforting me.

The mechanics were all gossiping about us in their gruff voices. Mr. Reyes wasn't gonna come out and tell them to knock it off, of course—too suspicious, too revealing of his involvement with us.

"You can't do this anymore," I said eventually.

"I can do whatever I want," Tony replied.

Huh. I thought he'd back down.

"Tony," I said, "you're all I have."

I just kept saying that, over and over.

Eventually my breathing settled. I pulled up my t-shirt to wipe my eyes and nose. Tony lifted me back up.

"Lover's tiff?" said the ugly greasemonkey from earlier.

"I should be so fucking lucky," I replied.

I took Tony's hand in mine and let us both away from

that place, forever.

—

Principal Estrada was a good guy. Divorced, balding, self-effacing. And definitely not stupid.

"How did you get your dad's signature?" he asked me, holding my forms up to the light.

I leaned back in my chair, getting leverage from placing one foot on the edge of his desk. "What can I say?" I held my hands up in a gesture of amazement. "I called OH EIGHT HUNDRED-FIND-DADDY. They connected me to him for the first time. I said, 'Dad, nice chatting finally, I would like to leave school because of a promising apprenticeship program I've signed up for. I even found a local business to sponsor me.' He was like, 'Cool, Son. I love you, Son. Good luck, Son.'" I made phones of my right and left hands and alternated them to my head, to indicate who was talking when. "I said, 'Thanks, Dad. I love you too. Nice to finally connect.'"

Estrada laughed sadly. He knew how badly I'd felt at school. I knew he felt like he'd somehow failed me. But, like, what the fuck? Bullying was timeless, shits were everywhere. And Estrada was just one guy. A guy I quite liked in fact. It's like Tony told me: it must take a specific hardened mind and deliberately positive outlook to survive an ordinary life. A self-deprecating sense of humour. A continual choice to see the paths of fate as funny. To feel relief at your lack of control.

Estrada shook his head and said "Well then. Godspeed."

I was determined to live an ordinary life myself. Not because I didn't aspire to greater, but because I didn't see typical aspirations *as* greater. Given what I'd seen—Mom, Tony, Jackson et al, the choices you have to make in adulthood—the mere act of living life *was* living life to its fullest. Like Tony said: No gradients.

I got up and headed to the door.

"You could have a bright future," he said eventually.

I turned to him. "It's looking brighter already!"

And that's how I got out before shooting the place up.

I often wondered why no one else did either.

But I guess, like me, in the end they figured it wasn't worth it.

—

I have never felt such relief before or since.

I just kept looking at the sky, thinking, It's done, it's over, I'm out, I'm free, I made it, I can breathe again.

And in the months that followed, whatever happened was almost irrelevant. I was out the frying pan and into the whatever the fuck else.

But during those times I had few shifts lined up, and I was alone too long, a new type of melancholy would set in. I would not resort to Mom's solution—and so road trips with Tony became an increasingly important distraction.

Post-escape-plan, our trips became more frequent and aimless. I'd throw empty forties out my window, smashing them along the highway while Tony played me videos from his phone.

We'd stop off places, sit on the car roof, stare up at the stars, and shoot the shit. Mostly about weird stuff we'd seen online. Tony always showing innocent memes from Gay Instagram about drinking too much, gossiping and being a lazy slut.

As for me, maybe to cope with the whole school thing, I'd developed a taste for gore. A guy chopping his own dick off, or sitting on a glass and having it smash in his rectum and bleed everywhere. All kinds of scat porn. Believe it or not, Tony appreciated my descriptions. He had an intense fascination for what I'd seen, but no desire to see it himself.

"The plentiful nature of it all amazes me," he said once while flipping the tops off two beers for us with a keyring. "I know why we should guard ourselves from it—and yet it is happening all the time, isn't it? While you work at BudgetBarn or I'm out sucking some guy's dick in a back alley, there are brutal murders and horrible accidents in this same world of ours. And while it does us no good to think about it—we're manipulating our world view when we refuse to look at it, no?"

A fun speculation. But I protected him from the worst

of it. Beheadings, self-filmed suicides. The murder of those Scandinavian women in Morocco. Those Ukrainian maniacs who went on a killing spree with blunt objects. Because I knew—just intuitively—that there were degrees of gore and I'd gone off the deep end.

"Then again," he'd continued that night, probably having seen the sly smirk on my face, "I wouldn't go get myself attacked on purpose just to broaden my life experience. Some people are just unlucky. Maybe there's nothing to be gained from delving further into it than that."

"You balance me out, man." I accepted a beer from him, smiling softly.

It was true. I was a different guy when I was watching, I don't know, the reflection of fireworks in Tony's eyes, their rainbow lights across his glossy lips. Tony's hand undulating in the highway wind's caress. Tony sunbathing by Lake Tahoe in his little Lycra shorts, jutting hipbones, pale skin almost translucent, marbled with delicate blue veins, the lake beyond him mirroring the gently scudding clouds in the cerulean sky. Tony, lying between my legs on the bonnet of my car, me lying back on the windshield, both of us speculating about our big bold futures—me a rockstar, him some sort of brand influencer, I was hardly ever listening—while we watched the sun go down.

He was my stand-in girlfriend; I, his stand-in

boyfriend.

The best both of us had.

For now.

—

After Tony told me about selling his virginity, I'd driven him home in silence. He went off to his trailer, I to mine.

Mom had passed out in front of the TV again. I took the ashtray off her armrest, with its smoking cigarette ready to burn the place down. Took the handle of vodka off the seat beside her, just before it spilled onto the couch.

I head straight to bed, staring at the ceiling. A big vinyl sticker coated it, giving it a mahogany wood effect that fooled no one.

Tony *knew* I thought he could do anything he wanted.

But *was* this what he wanted?

I took my shattered phone out and typed in his number. It was the only one I knew by heart other than 911.

He answered, silent at first.

"I'm coming with you," I told him.

"You're *what?*"

"When it happens. For your safety."

"No, you're not."

"I'm not asking, Tony. I go where you go."

He sighed deeply, his breath crackling through the phone. "I can't do this to you."

"And I can't watch you do this to yourself." I placed a hand on my chest as if to steady my heartbeat. "But that's not gonna stop this from happening, is it?"

"You ever think we know each other too well?"

We were silent together. I could feel him out there, in the trailer opposite mine. But still I needed this distance, needed not to see him in order to secure this deal. It was just a little less real over the phone.

I owed this to him, didn't I? He had used his body to protect me from harm. Now it was my turn to do it back.

"I'd do anything for you, man," I said eventually. "Even watch you get fucked by an old guy for money."

Really, I felt I didn't have the right to look away from it anymore. If this is what he'd been doing to spare me from bullying—to save my life and potentially the lives of others—I should look upon it. Like, if you want hotdogs and chicken nuggets, you should probably watch some cunt bleed out a pig or toss birds into a blender or whatever the fuck. Trace the barbarism to its source.

"Then I promise you this, Ryan. I'll get us both out of Eastbrook."

"I don't need you to do that, Tony. I just need you not to get murdered."

—

I sat on Tony's bed with him, on his laptop, as he showed me the advert he'd set up. The door to the room was open, naturally, Mr. and Mrs. Sun having always suspected we

145

were a couple.

The site he'd put it on was bizarre. Some escort page overpopulated with headless torsos, to which Tony had added his own.

In his photo, he was in a white jockstrap, laid down on his bed, photo taken with his phone above his head, but with his head cut off. I rotated the laptop around. The photo was kinda upside down, running from his neck at the bottom to legs at the top. More confusing than sexy.

Weirder still was the bidding war going on to possess this upside-down body for the very first time.

Once it hit midnight, we learned the final sum.

"Jesus, Tony. If the plan was to make enough to get you through Cal State, that'll do it."

He scoffed. "Cal State? This'll get me through Stanford three times over."

—

Tony and I stood outside the Hillcrest Motel, a run-down place off the I-5, beside nothing else but trees.

Crickets chirped all around. A gentle breeze hugged us with the day's last warmth.

I looked at the soft evening light on Tony's face. The quiet, the stillness suggested peace, not the gratuitous act of Tony's transactional agreement.

"Sure you wanna go through with this?" I asked him one last time. Whatever his answer, I would make it work.

"Yeah, man," he said, bumping me with his elbow.

"I'm all prepped." He jumped a little to make his tiny Gucci-esque backpack jiggle, in which he'd packed lube and condoms.

"Ugh. TMI."

I didn't have the right to say that, really. I'd sat outside his bathroom while he 'douched and stretched'—again, just in case anything went wrong, like he got something stuck up himself. Better me fishing around in there than his parents.

A limo showed up, and out came the highest bidder.

Dark suit, white shirt. No tie, collar unbuttoned. His head looked like it had been inflated out the top of his shirt the way the material squeezed his neck from every angle, all pinkish gathering folds of skin. Stubble, thinning white hair, muddy brown eyes, and greying skin.

He walked confidently, gave airs of being someone important. To be the kinda guy who would pay for something like this, you'd have to be a bored rich cunt, right? Who else would bother?

He looked back and forth between us. "What's this? Two-for-one deal?"

I rolled my eyes. "Hands off, old-timer. I'm just here to keep you from murdering my friend."

"A—Apologies, Sir!" Tony said, holding an arm out in front of me.

The man said nothing more as he walked past us towards reception.

We trailed behind.

"What are you doing?" He frowned. "Don't follow me. Go wait over there."

In he went alone. Tony and I looked at one another and shrugged.

—

The guy explained his plan when he called us. He'd found a room at one end of the motel and wanted us to climb in the window from the parking lot when no one was looking.

Whatever. He was the one paying. He probably could have had Tony cartwheel naked up the hallway towards him if he wanted.

Sure enough, he'd opened the window to room 385. I went in first, checking that the room was clear of dangerous or weird shit.

It was scuzzy and smelled like old man already. Stained wallpaper, cathode ray TV hanging off a broken mount in one corner. The wrinkled sheets on the double bed looked unwashed. I half-expected it to have one of those coin-operated vibrating functions. I never knew if those were real or just a running gag on TV.

I knew the guy wanted a discreet location—but really rich dicks like this guy had access to all that *Squid Game* bullshit, did they not? Moneyed titties, disco ball masks, velvet cloaks, bowls of Viagra, and organ music?

I know it's just a series but come on—they do that

shit, don't they? But they do it clean and classy.

All this motel scuzz, I reckoned, had to be part of this guy's fantasy.

He stood there in the distant corner, by the door, probably to help us feel safe as we came in. But the room was so dark, and he was so still, that it was like one of those horror movies where you'd blink and he'd be crawling along the ceiling towards you.

I turned, stuck a hand out the window, and beckoned Tony to enter. I then found myself a chair in the corner to sit in. It creaked precariously, as if threatening to collapse—but didn't. I sat back, leaning on one elbow, hand on chin, and let Tony get to work.

He took out his phone, attaching a little card reader dongle to its base. The man dutifully took out his card and swiped it.

"Take off your clothes, please?" Tony requested like an experienced masseur. He was not himself but a character now.

Smart. After all, the guy had only paid for Tony from the neck down.

The old guy obliged. Shoes, jacket, belt, shirt, trousers. Tony waited patiently, taking each item from him and folding it loosely on the writing desk beside me.

The guy took off his vest and boxers, letting them slip to the floor. So far, this was like a weird doctor's exam.

Tony stripped next, down to his white jockstrap. The type of underwear and its colour had been specified by this gentleman.

I smirked. I wanted to chide Tony for having no ass whatsoever. No meat or muscle, just bone. Like me at the peak of my bullying, when I couldn't keep any food down.

But the old guy was into it. I could see his dick, amidst the unshaven greying pubes, twitching.

I leaned back in my chair, arms over the rests, one leg crossed over the other, eyes narrowing. I was like some sort of umpire for the sugar daddy olympics.

Tony had the guy lie down on the bed, with his legs over the end.

I was about to witness what Tony had done so many times for both of us. At the same time, all I could think was that I wanted to take my boy out for a celebratory burger or three after this. Even if just to get the taste of old dick out of his mouth. I didn't like to see him wasting away like this. No matter who was into it. No matter how much they'd pay.

In a swift and practiced move, Tony kneeled between the guy's legs, took his dick in his mouth, and started sucking.

I watched in amazement. My boy was a master sucker. The tongue action in time with the lip movement, the head bobbing. The last time I'd been in awe of such mastery was at a warehouse rave, high on coke and ketamine, staring at the DJ as he held headphones up to one ear, syncing up the songs, switching from one to the next. Such acts took practice, yeah, but also an innate sense of timing that was beyond me.

Tony took the old guy's whole dick in his throat—it had expanded to a decent, perhaps above-average length.

Maybe life wasn't so bad that we had these primal pleasures at hand—drinking, drugging, fucking, and sucking. Maybe that was the point and everything else was bullshit. And my boy here could dispense not just pleasure but a type of care and intimacy that made others feel deeply recognised. He did it so willingly, so authentically, to complete strangers.

Yeah, my boy had a gift.

As Tony gasped, coming up for air—his face flushed, lips gone bright red—a weird feeling, like dread—envy, maybe, or fear?—washed through me.

And it hurt, near physically! Like the uncertainty of going to school when Jackson's gang had stopped bullying me and I didn't know what was coming next. But worse! A dull throbbing agony through every molecule of mine.

As the feeling crept through my crotch, I could feel it stir, twitch alive, to action.

I was getting hard.

I was getting cucked!

Another wave of dread: Oh no. Am I like that?

Followed by shame at the dread: Maybe I am a bit. Who gives a fuck?

The old guy began to moan.

"Ah, fuck," I said.

Tony paused, the length of the guy down his throat. He didn't want to acknowledge me but surely wondered what was so wrong that I had made a sound.

I shook my head at the old guy. "You fucking came already, didn't you?"

Tony extracted the dick and turned to me. "Ryan!" he shout-whispered, shooting me evils.

I scolded Tony: "You should have gone gentler on him. Imagine how long it's gonna take him to 'recharge!' How awkward it'll be." I gestured to the guy, who was still panting like he was coming. "And what are we gonna talk about in the meantime? The fucking stock market?"

But the guy's dick, while twitching, ran dry.

"Hm. Not got it in him anymore," I reasoned, folding my arms.

I got closer, examining him from one corner of the bed. His eyes were rolling around, arms twitching like he was trying to move but couldn't.

His moans were not sexual. They were in pain.

Tony looked at me. "Do you think he's…?"

I placed a hand on the guy's chest, on the sparse white hairs between his flattened pecs. His heart was thumping at a wild rhythm. "Having a heart attack?"

"Do you know CPR?"

"Fuck do you think?" I said. "Say he survives it, first he's gonna sue us for breaking his ribs, then for defamation. I'm not touching him."

"That's negligence!"

"Then call an ambulance!"

Tony looked around, like he'd just landed here in a dream. "But I can't be caught here."

"Then fuck off! I'll say I was blowing him."

"You can't, it'll go on your record!"

I stroked my chin. "Will it? I thought it was only illegal to buy sex."

Tony narrowed his eyes. "Pretty sure it's buying and selling, here."

"Huh." I headed over to the window, expecting Tony to follow. "All I know is that this is over."

"Wait."

I sighed. "What?"

Tony scratched at his neck. "I, uh—I sold something else."

I went bug-eyed in horror. "I'm not fucking a dude's corpse, Tony!" I had one leg out the window by now.

"What? N—no, I mean a—a video."

"A video?"

Tony stroked his arm, self-soothing. I looked him up and down. At his sad little jockstrap, elastic barely clinging to his slim frame.

I gestured to the dying guy. "Did he know about this 'video?'"

"Yeah."

I nodded. "Just me in the dark, then, again." I cracked the window open further, ducking my head out.

He ran over to me, grabbing my arm. "Please! A—a number of paying people are gonna be expecting—evidence. And if they don't get it, They'll—raise a fuss."

Oh. Oh fuck. I understood the predicament now.

"Okay," I said to Tony, climbing back into the room. "Then this is what we're gonna do."

—

A knock on the motel room door.

Tony, dressed once more, went to open it.

In came another confident old guy in a suit. This one was gaunt-looking—hollow cheeks, general sucked-out appearance—and had a curly moustache he'd clearly dyed brown.

Tony swiped his card on the phone dongle.

"What's this?" The new guy said, seeing me. "A two-for-one deal?"

"Save it," I said, pointing to Tony. "There's your twink. Have at it."

Tony set up his phone on the dresser, hands shaking. "Forgive my friend," Tony said. "He's just here for my protection."

"I'm wondering," the new guy said, pacing around. "Why did you call me at the last minute if I was the winner?"

"You were the runner-up, actually," Tony said.

This was part of our story—and it was true—but Tony was terrified. He'd only ever kept secrets from me—lied by omission—but never, to my knowledge, outright fabricated something.

"The real winner," Tony said, squeezing his hands into fists, "dropped out—at the last minute."

"Shh shh," this old guy said, cupping one hand behind Tony's head, the other running a long, wizened finger over my boy's lips. "Don't be afraid. I'll be gentle with you."

God, this was all more than I could take. I was almost in tears. Must have looked a state.

"What's up with you?" the guy asked. "Never seen a twink destroyed before?"

Fucking hell. This was turning into a bigger ask of me than I'd anticipated.

Tony took a neon pink balaclava from his backpack and put it on, looking like the world's least threatening bank robber.

He propped his phone on the writing desk and turned it on, getting the video mode open and hitting record.

I twitched, about to reach out and warn Tony that he was coated in a unique signature of easily identifiable tattoos. But there was no way of saying that in front of the fogey without sounding suspicious. And assuming everything went to the new plan, it wouldn't really matter.

So I sat back down in my chair and got ready to watch once more.

Tony had gone pale. He had the guy strip again, but you could tell his professional mask was slipping—even through the thick wool of his balaclava. The old guy frowned, perhaps expecting more confidence from Tony.

"Fuck did you expect?" I said to him, tutting. "You bought a virgin, not an expert."

The stripping routine repeated—and it was just as Tony was back down to his jockstrap, and the new old guy was lying down naked on the bed, that the ironing cupboard fell open and the first old guy's corpse flopped onto the carpet like a beached dolphin.

The alive old guy sat up, looked to the body, then to the twink kneeled between his legs.

Finally, as he heard me cock my Beretta, he turned to me.

And I was the last thing he ever saw.

———

"Tony? Tony!"

His jaw was slack. He stood upright, stiff and wide-eyed like a meerkat.

"Get over here. Keep your eyes on me."

He ran to me, holding me tightly—more out of fright

than appreciation, I was sure. I wrapped my arms around his sylph-like body, his marble-smooth skin. Again, my groin stirred—must have been the excitement, the fear, the adrenaline coursing to the wrong places.

I couldn't help but look at the corpse myself. This would be the worst thing I'd ever witness, if you discounted all my online research. Maybe when God fascinated me with gore, this was his plan. Now I needed to know: How did the real thing compare?

You had the smell of it for one. The burning iron, smoke and raw meat of it. Plus, the bad old man breath and unwashed skin.

I was close to vomiting, but I managed to hold it back. I even suppressed the noise of my attempted retchings, because I thought it might set Tony off. It hurt my chest to hold back the reflexes like that, my body telling me, *It's not a good idea to keep this in.*

My reflexes didn't know about DNA testing!

I caught the sight of myself in the full-length mirror on the wall. The blood sprayed across me, contrasting nicely with Tony's unblemished skin. I was Tony's battered side. I'd keep collecting our scars and injuries, like the crater-impacted moon protecting the Earth.

I leaned back to look into Tony's eyes once more. "Keep your focus on me, okay?" I knocked his phone over so it recorded only the table. We'd delete the footage later obviously, whatever.

"But what are you—"

Bang.

Tony's eyes went even wider. Too curious to see what I'd done, he ignored my command and turned to look at the carpet.

I'd shot the first old guy in the head.

"Are you nuts?" Tony whispered.

Nuts? No, I was quite proud of what I'd already dreamt up.

I knelt by the second old guy and picked up his hand. "Two lovers in an argument," I said. "One shot the other, then himself." I took the gun and placed it in the second guy's hand. "I can tell by the way he grabbed you that he's right-handed."

"But—"

I stood back up, raising a finger in the air. "I know what you're thinking. That they'll consider the angle of a shot when they try to figure out if it was a murder-suicide. Or that they'll find out the first guy's cause of death was a heart attack an hour before he was shot. But that's only if the cops feel like doing a good job."

I wanted to invite him to look at the scene again, to help my next point land—but I knew Tony was squeamish.

I held Tony by the shoulders and met his eyes. In my most soothing voice I said, "It's two old fags. I mean, I'm not saying that—but the *police* will. They'll be like, 'I'd rather do this than have my wife find out what I was up to,' you know? They'll find this scene *humiliating.* They'll be *dying* for an easy explanation. They won't give enough of a shit to do a good job."

"That's—that's..." Tony caught his breath as he considered his response. "I know you're excited about your theory, but you don't need to sound so jazzed about apathy. Besides…"

He trailed off as he looked to his phone, where it lay on the table.

Did he mean what I thought...?

I lifted his phone, like a bereaved loved one peeling back a sheet to identify the deceased.

It wasn't a recording.

It was a livestream.

—

Once Tony was fully dressed again, we crawled back out the window, round the back of the motel. It was nighttime now, sky turning navy, bordering on black. Dark clouds shifting moodily to the east. Under other circumstances, I might have appreciated its beauty.

I could hear the screams, murmurs and cries now. Voices echoed around. They must have gathered in the front parking lot.

Tony and I kept our heads down, scurrying along the motel wall, beneath the view of the rooms, warm light from their windows glowing mildly.

The motel's rear exit opened before us. We pressed

along the wall harder, waiting in the shadows. There was a man's hand on the door, holding it open, about to emerge. I would never learn why, but he thought better of it, softly closing the door once more.

We dashed over to my car. I got behind the driver's seat, Tony in the passenger's, and I pulled out of there.

—

We drove north, probably hours, didn't know how many, didn't want to know. It was definitely the longest I'd been in Tony's company without one of us speaking.

I was close to speeding the whole way, but not quite—at least when I remembered I should know how fast I was going. I opened the glovebox latch at some point, tossed my Beretta in there. No point in leaving it behind, now that no one would believe my masterful tableau. Apart from that I was zoned out, focused on the worn yellow road markings, my headlights revealing two slim white cones of expressway before us.

Eventually I pulled into a seemingly abandoned expressway rest stop. All but a handful of streetlights were off. It looked like there used to be a garage here, but the windows were boarded up, graffitied over.

"Okay," I said finally, running my hands through my hair. "That was definitely illegal."

"What," Tony said, "shooting that guy?"

I turned to him. "Both of them, I think. Second guy for desecration of a corpse. Or something like that."

LEO X. ROBERTSON

Here I thought I'd avoided a path of violence when I got out of school before shooting it up. Why, incidentally, had I thought someone else might? I didn't know of other bullied kids. I guess sometimes I'd just hoped there were, didn't want to suffer alone. Still, I hadn't wanted to end up like my bullies, resorting to violence. I'd wanted to double down on being nothing like them.

As if, as always, what I wanted had anything to do with anything.

"Why bring up the legality of what just went down?" Tony asked.

"Oh, you know," I said. "Because earlier we were debating whether it was negligent to let someone die of a heart attack. And just before that, whether it was illegal to sell sex or just buy it."

"Huh. Yeah. Simpler times."

Did it hurt to discuss this, by making it feel real again? Or did it help by reminding us both that yeah, that just fucking happened?

Tony was scrolling through something on his phone. I glanced over, and he held the screen up to me. It was his bank account, with the money from both the old guys. "Probably not going to Stanford now though."

"You kidding me?" I took the phone from him, staring at all those green zeroes. "I bet the Dean's son hunts golfers for sport."

Tony laughed. This wasn't his standard ironic

response though. It was hysterical.

He punched the ceiling. "Fuck!" Tears ran down his face in big shimmering rivulets.

"Tony," I said, panting, closing my eyes tightly, "if I don't say this now, I'll lose my nerve forever. You have to let me drop you off somewhere. Tell the cops I did this." I felt the sting of tears building in my eyes. "You always had a future. I never did. So, let's stop pretending otherwise."

I felt him squeezing my arm. "I go where you go," he said, quoting me back to myself.

I looked to him. In the glow of a single buzzing streetlight someone had forgotten to decommission, I watched sweat drip down his neck. I felt the heat of him in the air. I smelled his skin. Heady, sweet. Almost too much.

I wondered if Tony had ever been as real to me before as he was then. So viscerally, throbbingly right-in-front-of-me.

I reached out slowly, curling my fingers behind his head. He let me. He closed his eyes and pressed his cheek against my hand.

I gently pulled him closer and pressed our lips together.

I don't know why. Maybe just to stop him crying.

He worked his magic, pressing his lips tightly to mine, breathing deeply, tongue slipping in between my teeth. His plastic tongue piercing bent in my mouth. He'd told tales of its effects on certain men. Today I'd seen it firsthand.

As I kissed him back, I wondered how many virginities we had left in us. The Cherry Poppers, the papers would call us. Tony and I, we'd do Sacramento proud. It had been too long since its last serial killer. Maybe it had picked us for the job. A place as bleak as this must generate acts like ours. We were just a tiny part of its grand, unknowable ecosystem.

Blood coursed through me, all my pathways opening up and flooding with warmth, from my core to the tips of my fingers, toes. Head. Dick.

I pulled back out the rest stop parking lot, merging back onto the I-5, ripping along God knew where.

Tony cracked his window and lit up a joint. I'd once thought we were each other's best for the moment. I knew now we were the best we'd ever have.

'You're all I have.' Hadn't I kept repeating that, hysterical, outside the garage that one time?

I remembered something else about that day. When I'd repeated those words enough times, like an incantation, a new phrase had come to me. I didn't understand it at the time, so I didn't say it.

Now, it made perfect sense.

You're all I have, Tony.

So let me have you.

THE MOTH & FLAME

"Did any of that happen to you?" Luis asked.

Ben shook his head. "For better or worse, my own teenage years were nowhere near as interesting. But I wish I'd had a best friend I could look out for like that."

"Hm." Luis flicked at a teaspoon, letting it spin on the tablecloth. "And you let your dad read that?"

"What's wrong with that?" Ben replied.

"N—Nothing. He's—he was your dad. I guess."

Ben scooped more chocolate goop into his mouth. "It's all far less graphic than what I heard he got up to with minors. He was an evil, sadistic prick."

"Allegedly."

"Ha!" Ben clapped a hand to his mouth. In his incredulity, he'd spat chocolate onto the table. "I'm going to jail for manslaughter at least. What's one missing 'allegedly' on my rap sheet?" He used an Oliver Baring-esque non-sequitur to change topic: "What's your dessert?"

Luis looked to the second dessert, confused. "Mine?"

"Sit. Eat."

Luis sat shakily opposite him. "It's a—strawberry and white chocolate cheesecake."

"Sounds great. Enjoy."

Luis chopped into it with a dessert fork. "I've actually, uh, always wanted to try this." He scarfed down the mouthful greedily, getting cream on his face.

Ben leaned over, watching him carefully as he continued to eat. "At least you're not fired, huh?"

"What? Oh, your dad. Sure." Luis returned to the dessert, licking his lips. Luis caught his eye. "Why are you looking at me like that?" He held a fork out to Ben. "D—Did you want to try it?"

Ben leaned over, grabbing Luis' held-out wrist, pulling both of them back to their feet. He slipped an arm around Luis' waist and stuck his tongue out, licking the cheesecake from the waiter's lips.

Sirens, blaring closer, broke Ben's concentration.

As he pulled back and gazed into Luis' compliant yet petrified eyes, he wondered what the meaning of all these scripts was. All these stories. All this attempted escape.

Escape?

There was no escape.

Not really.

He looked to the floor at a perfect example.

See, you could stab your dad.

You could watch the life leak out of him with satisfaction.

You could lean over his dying body and tell him things you were too ashamed to say in times of peace.

But in the end, you still had to take him with you.

HATEFUL PITCHES

9 781998 763